The old man averted his eyes, unable to meet Gerard's uncompromising stare. He pored over the photographs again, then timidly pointed at the one labeled "Dr. Richard Kimble." "He mighta got out."

"Thank you," Gerard said sincerely.

"What the hell is this?" Rollins demanded. "A minute ago, you tell me he's part of the wreckage! Now you're telling *him*—"

Gerard ignored him. "Renfro—take that bus apart. Poole—set up operations here." He started moving down track, speaking as he went to the small army of Illinois State troopers and press that followed. "Ladies and gentlemen . . . our fugitive's been on the run for ninety minutes. Average foot speed over uneven ground—barring injury—is approximately four miles an hour, giving us a radius of six miles. I want a hard-target search of any residence, gas station, farmhouse, henhouse, doghouse, and outhouse in that area. . . .

THE
FUGITIVE

a novel by J. M. Dillard

based on the screenplay by Jeb Stuart and David Twohy
from a story by David Twohy
based on characters created by Roy Huggins

Island

ISLAND BOOKS
Published by
Dell Publishing
a division of
Bantam Doubleday Dell Publishing Group, Inc.
1540 Broadway
New York, New York 10036

ISBN: 0-440-21743-1

Printed in the United States of America

Published simultaneously in Canada

September 1993

10 9 8 7 6 5 4
OPM

For S.

THE
FUGITIVE

1

On the day Dr. Richard Kimble's world was destroyed, he had been running nonstop: from home to hospital to surgery to rounds without stopping for food or a moment's breath. He was accustomed to it and not at all tired, even though the day had been particularly hectic.

As he stepped from the cab onto the icy sidewalk, Kimble paused to stare up at the Chicago night sky. Wind swirled snow between the high rises; backlit by street lamps, flakes rained down, silent, dark silver, relentless. The sight made him recall lines from a short story by James Joyce that spoke of how the living were dissolving, falling away like the snow as one by one they slipped into death, to become memories.

Snowflakes, soft and cold, kissed his face, his

hands, and melted immediately. They were like nothing in the world. Able to be held and adored for only a short time before disappearing entirely from sight.

Kimble forced himself to the present and began moving again, cautiously making his way over the ice-covered sidewalk to the muddy, salt-strewn hotel entrance. With a smart salute, the doorman opened the glass door. Kimble nodded as he entered and was met by a blast of warm air that completely dissolved the remaining snowflakes on his coat and hair. He eschewed the elevator and dashed up the stairs, taking them two at a time, then checked his coat before moving into the cavernous ballroom.

The place was so noisy that he could scarcely hear the music or the announcer's voice, so crowded that he could barely glimpse the tops of the models' heads as they strolled the runway. But the banner over the rostrum was clearly visible: CHILDREN'S RESEARCH AND AID FOUNDATION.

A waiter he did not see thrust a glass of champagne into his hand. Kimble set it, untouched, on the first passing tray and craned his neck to scan the crowd. Locating Helen seemed hopeless.

"Richard . . . !" a deep voice exclaimed as a large hand gripped Kimble's elbow.

He looked into Jake Roberts's flushed, grinning face and coughed as he caught a lungful of cigar smoke. Jake was a big warm cheerful bear of a man, a surgeon who transcended the stereotype of the fussy, details-oriented egotist. He always managed to look rumpled, even on his best days, and wore his pants low beneath a swollen belly. Even in a tuxedo, he looked like a plumber, but none of his peers minded: Jake Roberts was one of the best pediatric surgeons in the country. Kimble could never get over seeing hands so huge work with such grace on such tiny patients.

Jake was talking around the cigar clenched in his teeth, but his words were swallowed up by the noise of the crowd. Kimble leaned closer, straining to hear.

". . . Cancún," Jake finished, as he steered Kimble toward a cluster of fellow surgeons at the bar. Trails of cigar smoke wafted lazily up from the group and hung above them in a cloud. "Nat just talked everybody into it . . ."

Nat Stein, the hospital equipment rep, stopped in the midst of taking drink orders from his companions and proffered Kimble a cigar. Nat was quick moving, dapper, and quite possibly the smarmiest person Kimble had ever met.

Kimble shook his head, his lips twitching faintly with ironic amusement. "So what's the deal? If the hospital buys ten new—"

"No, no, no . . ." Eyes wide with feigned sincerity, Nat raised a palm and swiped at the air as if to erase the very suggestion. "No strings attached, Dr. Kimble. Industrial Hospital Supply has no ulterior motives."

Jake Roberts guffawed.

Kimble jerked his head toward the bar. "On the house, huh?"

Nat nodded vigorously.

"Tonic water with lime," Kimble told the bartender, then cleared his throat and said, in a tone that cut through the other conversations: "You'll never get me to sell my soul for one of those trips."

Silence descended; the others regarded him uneasily. Stone-faced, Kimble took his drink, sipped it, then turned to wink at the aghast rep. "But if you get any more Bulls tickets, Nat, give me a call."

The group broke into relieved laughter—Nat's was the loudest of all. He took the opportunity to move off into the crowd and was immediately almost hit by the follow-through of an imaginary golf swing; only a swift reaction managed to keep his tonic water from sloshing down the front of his tux. The golfer was Dave Austin, one of the residents.

"You're slicing, Dave," Kimble told him. "Don't turn your hip."

Dave swiveled his head and grinned. "Thanks, Richard."

He managed a few more yards before he recognized Kathy Wahlund. She was standing on tiptoe watching the runway with her back to him, but he recognized her easily from the aging leather jacket she always wore. She turned briefly, frowning at the crowd without seeing him, and he grinned at the sight of her Grateful Dead T-shirt. Kathy had an M.D. but had gone into lab work rather than clinical practice because of her misfit's temperament; she refused to cover her T-shirt and jacket with a lab smock, and constantly ignored procedure, but her behavior was tolerated because of her brilliance. Kimble liked her because she was sincere and passionate (if incredibly outspoken) in her beliefs, and because he'd learned long ago that her sharp tongue and rebellious behavior were defenses erected to shield an overly tender heart.

Kimble moved to her left, stretched his arm behind her and tapped on her right shoulder, then pulled his hand away swiftly so that she turned to see no one behind her to the right. She figured it out, though, and jerked her head to the left, hair swinging, and clicked her tongue in annoyance when she saw him. But she could not quite manage to suppress a fleeting grin.

"I'm *so* glad you talked me into coming, Richard." Her tone dripped acidic irony as she peered back at the runway with undisguised disgust. "I can pick my cruise wardrobe."

Kimble's lips thinned in a small smile as his gaze followed hers. Kathy didn't get along with most people at the hospital for one reason or another, and she despised Nat Stein most of all. On their first encounter, she had called him amoral slime and heaved a file at him.

Nat somehow always forgot to make sales calls on Kathy.

Kimble gave her shoulder a "hang tough" pat. "It's for a good cause, Kath . . . Besides, you need to get out of the lab more. Your electron microscope is starting to give you a tan."

She made a grimace that was almost a smile.

Kimble moved on, scanning the crowd. Still no Helen, but he eyed a good friend a few heads down. "Hey, Charlie!"

Dr. Charles Nichols, head of pathology at Chicago Memorial Hospital, turned. Like Kimble, he was in his mid-forties, but still boyish, trim, and athletic. He grinned, his perfect teeth flashing white against a dark tan. Nichols was a skilled administrator, whose enthusiasm and energy had turned the hospital from a financially struggling institution into a thriving business.

"Richard!" Nichols reached through the crowd for Kimble's hand. "I just saw someone who wanted to meet you . . ."

He barely registered Nichols's words; he had picked Helen out of the crowd. He was surprised it had been so hard to do, as she seemed the most beautiful woman in the crowd to him, more striking than the runway models without any of the artifice. Dressed in a simple black evening gown with a single strand of pearls against her pale, delicate throat, she stood surrounded by a group of keenly interested male admirers, but the interest was clearly unshared. She seemed to sense her husband's gaze and glanced up to smile at the sight of him. To Kimble, the room seemed suddenly warmer, brighter, more inviting. His dark mood lightened considerably, but it still hovered in his mind like an uninvited guest.

He had not wanted to come, not really. He had wanted to stay home with Helen, and he knew that deep down, she had wanted the same. But they had encouraged one another, had spoken cheerfully of the benefit, of what a good organization CRAAF was, of all the children that would be helped.

Nichols's voice drew him back; he realized he was being introduced, and instinctively extended his hand.

"Richard Kimble . . ." Nichols was saying, gesturing toward each of the two men. "Alex Lentz."

Kimble grasped Lentz's hand and gave it a single firm shake. Lentz was young, mid to late thirties, smiling, and tan. Kimble knew he was an M.D. without asking. The name seemed vaguely familiar, and he assumed he had heard it before on another doctor's lips or seen it in a medical journal. Lentz could have been Nichols's clone, and probably dreamt of someday stealing his job.

"Alex is working on the RDU90 trials for Devlin-Macgregor," Nichols added by way of explanation.

"Dr. Kimble," Lentz began eagerly. "Sorry, we've been trading phone calls the last few days. Something about a biopsy report I returned to you?"

An alarm went off in Kimble's memory as he recalled where he had seen the name: on a pink WHILE YOU WERE OUT slip. He studied Lentz with sudden attentiveness. "Yeah . . . Three. Livers appeared hepatitic to me." He paused, then decided to say nothing more lest he embarrass the young doctor in front of Nichols. No point in saying anything to suggest Lentz had screwed up; it could have been a simple case of paperwork getting mistakenly swapped. But Kimble knew a badly damaged liver when he saw one, and he had seen three this week—in fact, he had joked with everyone else about the trend. You could go six months without seeing a particular ailment, and then in one week, you'd hit the jackpot and see half a dozen cases. Last week it had been kidney stones; this week, it was livers. Three clearly precirrhotic livers, three biopsy reports which said they were normal. And all of them participants in Lentz's drug study.

Lentz's smile stayed in place, but Kimble noted the sudden tension around the younger man's mouth and eyes. "I'll be in my office in the morning and I'll pull up the samples," Lentz offered cheerfully. "Is that a good time for you?"

Kimble nodded. "Sure."

Lentz held Kimble's gaze a few seconds longer; his expression hardened faintly, then warmed again as he faced Nichols. "See you, Charlie."

He made his way through the crowd. Kimble watched him a moment, then sought Helen's eyes again, but she had vanished. He began moving slowly toward the place he had last seen her.

Nichols walked alongside, fumbling in his pocket; at last he drew out a valet ticket and handed it to Kimble. "Before I forget, I went by the garage this afternoon and picked up the Ferrari. Thanks for the loaner again."

Kimble pocketed the ticket. "They fix it this time?" Nichols was forever buying sports cars which invariably spent more time at the mechanic's than they did on the road.

Nichols shrugged blithely. "We'll see."

Kimble raised his eyes heavenward with a long-suffering sigh, which was interrupted when he realized his wife was standing in front of him. He leaned down and kissed her. She took his hand and drew back to study his face with its graying beard; he saw the trace of concern in her eyes.

"You look fabulous." Nichols planted a perfunctory kiss on the cheek she presented him.

"Hello, Charlie." She smiled politely, but Nichols, his mind already on other things, had turned his attention back to Kimble and was talking.

"We've got a court tomorrow at three."

"I'll be there," Kimble replied, and Nichols gave them each a farewell nod and moved off into the crowd.

The silky fabric of Helen's gown brushed against Kimble's hand, and he reached out to stroke the soft flesh of her arm. So soft and so warm . . .

He thought suddenly of snow and felt an urgent desire to be away from crowds and noise and lights and laughter, away from everything except soft darkness and silence. He faced her, feigning boredom. "Well, I've seen everyone. Can we leave?"

"That would be a little abrupt, don't you think?" She turned full toward him as if he were the only person in the room and slowly lifted his hand to her lips and kissed it, then lifted it to her cheek. There was so much love and sorrow and comfort in that small gesture that Kimble would have done anything for her in that moment, would gladly have died in her place. In the hours and days and months that followed, he came to wish that he had.

For Helen's sake, he suffered through dinner, and began to seriously wonder whether sitting at home watching the Bulls wasn't a far more pleasant alternative to listening to such witless chatter. Then he corrected himself, and was sure. His wife was captured between two researchers and managed to maintain an interested expression as they recited the long boring details of their most recent studies, while Kimble listened to their wives' inane conversation.

"Where's your husband on staff?"

"My husband's an orthopod at Northwestern . . ."

"That's a marvelous dress you're wearing . . ."

"Do you like it? My husband says it's a 'four-fracture number . . .'"

After an hour of it, he caught Helen's eye, subtly motioned to his watch and mouthed *Now.*

She gave a barely perceptible shake of her head. Kimble rolled his eyes and lifted his head in a small gesture of exasperation, then went back to pushing his salmon in a kiwi and ginger cream sauce around his plate.

"I told my husband that he was going to kill us if he didn't stop operating," one of the younger wives, who'd had more than a few glasses of wine, announced loudly; the others at the table fell silent. "What with this AIDS thing, he's putting us all at risk."

Helen absorbed this comment without reaction, but Kimble saw the dimming of warmth in her eyes. She looked at her husband and mouthed the word *Now.*

"I'm sorry," she told her dinner partners with a smile. "I have to get my husband home."

Kimble rose gratefully, with what he hoped was not too obvious relief.

On the way out, they passed Nichols's table. As

Kimble shook his friend's hand, he glanced up to see Alex Lentz watching balefully from across the room.

Kimble's sense of relief increased on the drive home. The snow had stopped, leaving the city a sparkling, white-dusted jewel, and Helen nestled beside him and ran her fingers through his hair. He knew she was as happy as he was to have left the party.

"You looked handsome tonight," Helen murmured.

"Thank you." He glanced at her in the rearview and grinned.

She took the smile as a sign he had enjoyed the compliment a bit too much; he watched as, in the mirror, her eyes narrowed and filled with a playful light. "Uh, huh. Most men in a tuxedo look like waiters . . ."

"But me?" He cocked an eyebrow waggishly.

"You looked more like . . . a band director."

He stopped at a red light, leaned over, and kissed her.

After a long moment she pulled away and whispered breathlessly, "Are we home yet?"

He smiled at her, then glanced up to see the green light changing to yellow. He ran it and drove like a demon all the way home, he and Helen stroking each other and kissing and giggling like kids.

The instant they pulled up in front of the house, both the pager and car phone rang at once. He and Helen shared a look of resigned despair as he picked up the receiver and spoke into it. "Dr. Kimble . . ."

The voice belonged to Rhea Gates, one of the night-shift nursing staff. "Doctor. Sorry to bother so late, but Dr. Price asked me to call. He and Dr. Falawi could really use your help in the O.R.—"

Kimble leaned forward. "When?"

"Now. They ran into a bleeder. Sounds pretty hairy."

"Okay. Tell them I'll be there in ten minutes." He replaced the receiver in the cradle and gave Helen an apologetic look. "Tim's got a problem."

She kissed him, lightly running her fingers through his hair and down the side of his bearded cheek. "Call me on your way home," she said, and opened the door. As he waited while she made it up the steps and into the house, he saw the snow captured in the headlight beams. Flakes began raining down again, so fast and heavy this time that she was soon hidden from view by swirling white.

"**C**avalry's here." Decked out in scrubs, Kimble stuck his head into the O.R. to see Falawi and Price, both looking exceptionally harried, blink up at him above their masks. He retreated to the scrub room and started soaping up. Mohamed Falawi, Chicago Memorial's chief resident, came out and briefed him. Falawi was plump, dark-complected, with permanent dark circles beneath his black eyes; tonight, it seemed he had *two* purplish half-moons under each eye.

"Patient is a male, forty-three," Falawi said, with an exhausted sigh but intense concentration on the matter at hand. "We pulled his gallbladder and the bleeding started."

"What's his pro time?" Kimble asked.

Falawi released a glum little grunt. "He's at thirty-six seconds." Kimble did a double take at the news. "We've got a major bleeder in here."

Kimble finished soaping up to his elbows and began to rinse. "You talk to the family?"

The resident shook his head. "None. He's off the street."

Falawi helped Kimble on with his gloves and mask, then the two pushed through the swinging door to the O.R., where Tim Price and Josefina Munoz, the anesthesiologist, waited. The nurse was Marie Johnson, which cheered Kimble; Marie was one of the best and most experienced scrub nurses at the hospital. No one greeted him. The tension in the room was palpable, and all attention was focused on the man bleeding to death on the table.

The first thing Kimble noticed was the blood; the second, the fibrous, scarred, enlarged liver; the third, a homeless guy who seemed too well nourished and healthy for a street alkie at age forty-three—or for that matter, anyone with a liver that looked like his.

It took him less than a second to make these observations then sigh and tell himself that this was the week for mysteriously ailing livers, especially mysteriously ailing livers in anyone involved with Alex Lentz; in that same amount of time, he had figured out the location of the bleeding and how to deal with it.

"Okay," he said to Munoz. "I'm clamping. Can he tolerate it?"

Above her green mask, Munoz's dark eyes indicated uncertainty. "He's a very sick guy."

Kimble sighed. If they didn't clamp soon, the man would die. "Do we have a choice?"

Munoz sighed too. "Go for it."

"Marie," he ordered, without looking at her, "give me a clamp." He did not look at the instrument in his hand when she gave it to him, but knew from its weight and feel that it was the correct one. He set to work, probing gently, firmly through the bloody organs for the offending artery. The room grew silent; too silent for comfort. Kimble decided it was time to ease some of the tension.

"Your husband know you're here tonight, Marie?" he quipped, and beside him, she giggled. She was much older than he, stocky and straitlaced and prim, but the first time he'd said, "We've got to stop meeting like this," after a long night in surgery, she'd adored it. It had become their little joke.

His fingers found the bleeder and applied the clamp. Nothing to do now except wait. His tone of voice changed abruptly as he addressed Falawi and Price. "What about his liver?"

Falawi answered. "History's sketchy. Could be an alcoholic."

Something about it didn't ring true. Pursuing his suspicion, Kimble asked, "Who referred him?"

The answer from Falawi was precisely the one he expected.

"He's on a drug protocol. RDU90."

Lentz again—of course. Kimble had already spoken to Tim Price about this RDU90 and liver business; he and Tim shared a look.

"The wave of the future," Kimble said dryly, instantly returning his gaze to the clamped artery. The bleeding was easing, which meant they were dealing with only one bleeder. This was going to be easy, too easy, and then he would be able to go home to Helen. With a surge of good humor, he returned to teasing the scrub nurse. "Marie, have you told Frank yet?" Frank was Marie's husband; Kimble winked at Tim Price and said in a confidential tone, "Frank is so jealous of this late-night thing we've got going here . . ."

"You promised you were going to tell Helen first," Marie reminded him.

"Couldn't. It would break her heart." Kimble looked up at Tim. "This should hold him. Bleeding's stopped." He paused. "Let's get a biopsy of that liver." At Price's assenting nod, he turned to Marie. "Send it downstairs and make sure you get Kath a slice."

A slice would routinely go to Lentz, for his study results; he'd probably screw it up again and say the liver tissue was perfectly normal. It wasn't standard procedure to send an additional sample to Kath, but Kimble had been doing so ever since the first biopsy report from Lentz had come back. Not because he suspected Lentz was intentionally trying to fudge the reports—at least, he hadn't the first couple times it happened—but because he wanted someone competent like Kath to corroborate or challenge what he felt was unforgivably sloppy lab work. Of course, Kath was so swamped with routine work that she probably hadn't noticed the extra slides; but when she realized Kimble was having her duplicate work being done elsewhere, she'd have a fit.

Price looked up, his eyes and brow managing to convey considerable relief. "You staying for the closing, Rich?"

Kimble was already moving away from the table and shedding his scrubs. "No." He grinned, thinking of Helen waiting for him at home. "I got a date." He strode into the scrub room, tossed his hat and mask into the bin; behind him, the door opened. He swiveled his head to see Tim Price, still masked.

"Hey, Richard . . ."

Kimble turned.

Beneath his mask, Tim was smiling. "Thanks."

Kimble returned the smile and left. He was in a cheerful mood, he told himself, happy to be returning home to Helen. But in the back of his mind there remained a vague, growing uneasiness, one he would not fully comprehend for several months, and the name of it was RDU90.

Helen was still dressed when the phone rang, sitting downstairs reading with an afghan draped over her bare shoulders.

The phone's ringing broke the room's heavy, silent spell. She smiled as she picked up the receiver, and was gladdened by the sound of Richard's cheerful voice.

"Hi. I'm five minutes away . . ."

"That was fast. Were you able to help Tim?"

"Yeah. We had a bleeder, but it was a quick fix. The guy should pull through."

"I'm glad it went well." She lowered her voice seductively. "I'll see you in a minute . . ."

He didn't say a word, but she knew nonetheless that he smiled into the receiver. She hung up and snapped off the reading lamp, then started up the stairs.

It was on the landing, as she reached for the hall light, that her heart began to beat faster with an odd and growing fear as a chill ran up her spine. Against her conscious will, she glanced over her shoulder, expecting to see someone at the corner of her vision. Someone skulking in the shadows. . .

And saw only darkness. Helen turned on the light and moved into the bedroom, trying to shake the increasing sense of oppressive stillness, reminding herself that Richard would be home any minute to break the spell. She stepped into the walk-in closet, flipped up the light switch, and paused in the bright incandescent glow, thinking to undress . . .

No. Better to have Richard help her. She smiled faintly at the thought, and out of habit reached forward to pull shut a closet door, one Richard always left open.

What came next happened quickly, too quickly to understand, almost too quickly to react.

Movement. A blur. A hand, reaching out of the midst of the hanging clothes to clutch her neck, with such sudden force that the air was knocked from her in a gasp. She felt no fear: the adrenaline surge produced a reaction far beyond anything classifiable as emotion. Her body felt at once cold, hot, pulsating with a sheer electrical force that shot down her spine and blotted out all thought, all reason.

The pearls were driven into the delicate flesh at her collarbone as the hand squeezed, closing off her windpipe. She gagged, but made no sound, and began to claw at the hand at her throat, began to pull away. The necklace tangled in her flailing arms and broke, spilling pearls in a soft cascade of sound.

The attacker stepped out of the clothes into the light then, but her eyesight was already dimming and she saw nothing of him but a large, looming shadow. She renewed her efforts and somehow pulled free, and lurched gasping out of the closet into the bedroom, toward the phone on the nightstand.

She made it, and got her hand on the receiver.

There followed two short whines, soft and high-pitched at first, then abruptly loud and dull, both of them coincident with searing pain—the first, hot and bright in her thigh, the second, dull and hideous and bone-shattering in her skull.

She teetered, through some miracle of instinct managing despite her wounds to continue the movement and pick up the receiver—and then she was yanked backwards, and fell. The phone thudded onto the carpet beside her.

For a moment the world darkened. She saw nothing, knew nothing; then she blinked, and her eyesight cleared.

The shadow of her attacker wavered in the periphery of her vision, but she was not afraid anymore, would never again be afraid of anything; for out of the darkness she could see a warm inviting light beckoning her. She began to reach toward it.

2

The weather had worsened to near-blizzard conditions by the time Kimble pulled into the driveway and dashed into the house. The wind howled at the front door and he slammed it shut with difficulty, then pulled off his coat and shook the snow from it before hanging it in the foyer closet.

The living room was silent; he could hear the steady ticking of the grandfather clock. Kimble tossed his keys on the entry table and glanced at a stack of mail there.

"I'm home," he called up the stairs. "Did you hear who won the Bulls game?"

No answer. Helen had bionic ears—or so they joked—so he wondered whether she had dropped off to sleep immediately after speaking to him, but as he stepped into the kitchen, he saw the light on the wall phone.

Awfully late for a telephone call; he prayed it wasn't another emergency, but then, his beeper would have gone off. The washer buzzed as he paused to sort through the mail. He switched the laundry over to the dryer, started the machine, then opened the pantry door to peer at the wine rack. He chose a bottle he knew Helen was fond of, scooped a couple glasses from the shelf, and headed up the stairs.

The hall light was on. Three steps from the top, Kimble paused as his gaze caught something white and shiny on the carpet by his foot. Without thinking, he stooped over to retrieve it, and saw that it was one of Helen's pearls.

There was no reason for the sight to have terrified him—but as he straightened on the staircase, Kimble's heart began to pound. The silence emanating from the bedroom seemed suddenly ominous.

He angled his head, craning his neck so that he could see a small slice of the bedroom from where he stood. On the floor between the closet and the bed, a lampshade rested on its side.

He moved stealthily up the stairs, over the wooden landing to the bedroom doorway, and paused, motionless, not daring to breathe.

In the crack behind the half-open door, he saw the dark outline of a human form—a form too tall, too bulky to be his wife's. In the stillness he heard a man's ragged breathing and knew it was not his own.

The fear pumped adrenaline into his system with a

raw, primal, galvanizing force. He hurled his own body against the door with a strength he had never possessed before and never would again. It collided with a dull sound against flesh and bone and drywall; the figure hiding there yelped. Something shiny and metal fell from its grasp and struck the hardwood floor.

Kimble dived for the gun without thinking, only to be slammed to his feet by a thick forearm. The man—lumbering, graceless, of bullish build and strength—scrabbled for the weapon. Just as he reached it, Kimble grabbed an ankle and pulled with all his might. The man fell just as his fingers struck the gun, sending it skittering across the hardwood floor of the landing, and over the edge. There was a loud clatter as it struck the floor of the entry hall three flights below.

Sirens wailed in the distance.

The intruder kicked free of Kimble's grasp and ran toward the landing, but Kimble stayed right behind him and caught an arm before the man made it to the stairs. The arm felt odd, slightly cool to the touch, and when Kimble pulled, it twisted at an unnatural angle that would have caused a fracture under normal circumstances.

Kimble yanked harder, and the limb came free in his hands, detaching from the body at mid-humerus, between shoulder and elbow. It was hollow, the lining of the interior wired with electrodes. Kimble gaped at it in amazement, then looked up to see the man's startled face—olive-skinned, dark-eyed, framed with curling, dark hair—hovering above his.

And then the blur of a moving fist, and Kimble was knocked in the jaw. He staggered and fell backwards. Before he could recover, the man had taken his limb and fled down the stairs.

Outside, the sirens grew more insistent.

Kimble pulled himself to his feet, thinking to follow, but a whisper, faint and halting, came behind him:

"He's here . . . still in the house . . ."

He wheeled. On the other side of the bed, in a pane of light shining from the closet, lay Helen. She still wore her evening gown, which flowed out onto the floor around her, its black a sharp contrast to the deathly white of her skin. With one hand she clutched the phone receiver so that it lay on the floor near her lips; with the other, she held the side of her head.

An anxious, strident voice filtered through the mouthplate of the receiver. "Did I hear you right? Your attacker is still in the house? Ma'am?"

"He's trying to kill me," Helen said, in a whisper that was a scream. Her eyes were glassy, unfocused. Kimble stepped into her line of vision, and at the sight of him, the phone slipped from her weakening grip.

The loud voice came over the receiver again. "Will you repeat that, please . . . ?"

"Richard . . . He's trying to kill me . . ."

He knelt beside her. He had been in a thousand life-or-death emergencies and had never lost his composure, had always remained calm; it was the only way to save lives. But this was not a patient—

this was Helen, and he wanted to scream, to howl at the injustice of it all, to kill the man that had hurt her. For her sake, he struggled to contain himself, but when he reached out to touch her, his hand shook.

Her flesh was cool and soft and damp.

"My head," she moaned, and he saw the purplish red necklace of bruises encircling her neck. He stroked it tenderly, with trembling fingers, wanting to brush away the pain.

"Hang on, babe, it's going to be all right," he said in his best professional tone, and did a quick exam: bullet wound in the thigh. He didn't see that much blood, but it must have nicked the femoral artery, because her lips were graying and her breathing was rapid; she was going into shock. But why? He ran his hand over the silky fabric of her dress; it was dry except for a tennis-ball-sized spot. He pressed his palm against it hard to stanch the flow, but instinct and training told him she had to be bleeding from *somewhere else* . . .

"My head," she moaned, and flailed one-handed at him; he pulled his head back as her long nails scratched his face. She dug them into his arm. "Richard . . . my . . . hold . . . me . . ." Her eyes rolled away from his, toward some unspeakable horror on the ceiling. One hand still clutched the side of her head.

With sudden, sickening insight, Kimble realized where the bleeding had to be coming from. Gently, he peeled her hand away; it stuck to her scalp with congealing blood.

Beneath, the skull had been shattered to reveal its glistening gray-white treasure.

The phone on the floor beside Helen spoke. "Hello? You said his name is Richard? Ma'am? Can you talk to me? Ma'am?"

Kimble bowed low beneath the weight of blinding, mind-numbing pain. He gathered his wife in his arms and held her in an agony he had not experienced in three years, and had hoped never to again. And when he heard the splintering crash of the door being kicked in three floors below, and the shouts of the Chicago police identifying themselves, he could not call out, could not react. Did not care enough to react.

Movement. Thunder of a dozen feet upon the stairs. Kimble rocked Helen in his arms. He did not react when the cops entered with guns drawn to witness the bloody pietà, did not even look up until the first cop ordered:

"Move away from her!"

Only then did he raise his face; but even then he did not see them. He was gazing beyond them, through the bedroom window, at the cone of light cast by the shining streetlamp. At the white, relentless, falling snow.

They made him leave her. They made him leave her lying alone on the bedroom floor and took him down to the kitchen sink, where he washed his hands like an automaton. One of the officers took away his bloodstained tux jacket; another brought him a clean parka from the dryer.

There was no time to privately grieve. The townhouse filled with cops. Outside, the streets filled with police cars, curious neighbors, television newsvans. Forensics people came in and began dusting for prints, taking pictures—of Helen, of the bruises circling her neck, of her wounds, of the bedroom, of his own gun, still hidden in the bottom dresser drawer where he kept it. Cameras flashed until Kimble was blinded.

They asked questions. He answered. They led him out past the circus on the snow-covered street into a waiting police cruiser and drove him to the police station, to the Eleventh Street District House.

He was led into a small room with three chairs and a desk. Two men came in and introduced themselves as Detectives Kelly and Rosetti. He remembered little of Rosetti, who watched quietly for most of the interrogation; Kelly was overweight, aggressive, approaching open hostility. Kimble sat through most of the questioning with his hand to his face, staring down at the grimy desk, at the dirty floor, at Helen's gaping head wound; staring down at invisible snow.

The interview went on for hours; the interview went on forever. He could not remember most of the questions he was asked that night, but a few of them stuck in his memory:

What kind of gun did he have?

"It was . . . a thirty-eight, I think. I only saw it for a second. I knocked it out of his hand."

Do you own a gun, Dr. Kimble?

"Yes."

What kind of gun?

"A thirty-eight Smith."

Did you have your key with you tonight, Dr. Kimble?

"Yeah, of course . . ."

Your wife was loaded, wasn't she? I mean, she was worth quite a bit of money . . .

He had looked up at them then, with disbelief that swiftly turned to outrage. He had lowered his hand from his face and leaned forward in the unyielding wooden chair, peering first into Kelly's unreadable face, then Rosetti's. "What's going on here? This guy was trying to *rob* us."

Cold stares. Immovable disbelief.

Kimble's lips parted; he exhaled a breath as if he had been kneed in the chest. "You guys have got to be out of your minds. *I didn't kill my wife!*"

He rose, beyond anger, beyond indignation, and took a step toward the door. The uniformed officer who had been standing watch there moved quickly to block his path. Kimble wheeled to glare at Kelly, whose lips curved ever so slightly.

Let's start over, Dr. Kimble. What did you have for breakfast?

They booked him that night in his tuxedo shirt and black tie. He should have called Helen's family and closest friends to break the news himself, to weep with them a time. Instead, he made one two-minute phone call, to his attorney, Walter Gutherie. He had to look Gutherie's home number up.

Gutherie nearly hung up on him. It was predawn, and Walter's voice was thick with sleep. "Who is it?"

Kimble tried to speak, tried to summarize what had transpired that evening in one coherent, rational sentence, and bowed his head in grief.

"God *damn* it—"

"Walter. Don't hang up. It's Richard Kimble."

"Richard?" His "this-had-better-be-good" tone changed abruptly to one of concern. "Richard, you sound like hell."

He choked getting the words out. "Helen's dead. She . . . she was killed . . . Murdered . . ."

"My God," Walter whispered. A long silence followed. Gutherie was not close enough to the family to be wakened in the middle of the night with the news, and he knew it.

Several seconds passed before Kimble could bring himself to speak again. At last he drew in a long, shuddering breath. "Walter, they're charging me."

Gutherie was suddenly keenly alert. "Where are you?"

"A police station. I don't . . . I don't remember which one."

"Eleventh Street," the cop standing beside Kimble said.

Gutherie heard it. "I'll be right there."

* * *

They put him in Cook County Jail without bail. They stripped him of his tux and gave him neon lockup fatigues to wear; they took his watch and wedding ring and sealed them in plastic bags. To Kimble, it seemed merely that his outer circumstances had changed to express his inner. He lay awake nights on the narrow, lumpy mattress that offered no rest, reliving Helen's final moments, reliving the encounter with the one-armed man, reexperiencing the pain in hopes of coming up with some small piece of evidence that would free him. When he did fall asleep, he dreamed of holding Helen in his arms. Watching Helen die. Feeling the life drain from her.

He would wake from the dream to the nightmare.

The jail proved hell was indeed a temporal phenomenon: it was crowded, grim, devoid of any sign of human pleasure or comfort; it smelled of piss and sweat and cold concrete. When Kimble asked Walter Gutherie about the bail situation, Walter shrugged and muttered something about it being an election year and the judge wanting to show he was tough on crime.

The court docket was overloaded. Weeks dragged into months. Winter changed to spring, then summer. When Kimble's trial finally came up, Walter Gutherie filed motions to extend in an effort to buy more time to prepare.

More time to find the one-armed man. Kimble always asked how the investigation was going; Gutherie always replied evasively.

It was at a meeting a few days before the trial that

Kimble first realized he would lose. Gutherie and his eager young assistant, Randolph, met him in the prisoner interview room. As always, Gutherie did most of the talking; as always, Gutherie most times would not meet his eyes. That day, Kimble began to understand why.

When the guard escorted Kimble into the interview room, Gutherie was staring out the window at the jail yard; Randolph, still young but no longer eager, stared at Gutherie. Walter glanced over as Kimble sat, graced him with a swift nod, then went back to looking out the window as though he were studying Kimble's future. He did not smile. Neither Gutherie nor Kimble did much smiling in those days.

Gutherie cleared his throat and launched into what was clearly a rehearsed speech. "We've had private investigators interview over a hundred amputees, Richard. We can't find this guy."

Kimble stiffened at his attorney's tone; it carried the same message as the tone used by Detective Kelly on the night of Helen's murder: disbelief. A muscle in his jaw began to spasm. "I know what I saw, Walter."

Gutherie sighed and pressed a hand against the window. "I put you on the stand to say what you saw without anything that remotely smells like proof, and the state's attorney is going to take this one-armed-man story and run it up our ass."

Kimble's lips parted in outraged amazement, then began to form the word: *Story . . . ?!*

Gutherie didn't give him a chance to say it. He wheeled, and for once held Kimble's gaze. His eyes were hard. "Look, Richard, you're paying us a lot of money to defend you. A plea to second-degree—"

"You don't believe me," Kimble whispered, aghast, and looked away, closing his eyes. At that instant, he understood: The pain of losing Helen, of knowing the man who murdered her walked free, had not been enough. *He* was going to be punished for it. He was going to prison. His own attorney was convinced of his guilt. He felt a surge of raw emotion that was not rage, not grief, not horror, but was all three. He turned back to Gutherie and said vehemently, with gritted teeth: *"I didn't kill my wife."*

Gutherie just looked at him blankly, then turned his face and went back to staring out the window. His tone was hard. "You're a successful upper-middle-class white man charged in a violent crime. It's a circumstantial case, but it's also a jury trial. We play 'em, they play 'em . . . But if we lose, we lose big." He glanced over his shoulder at Kimble. "Just remember, they're lined up a block long to have your hide."

The trial began in late summer, and continued through the fall. For the courtroom appearance, they let him dress in a suit Walter had finagled from the townhouse, and they gave him the small plastic bag that held his wedding ring. When Kimble first entered, the head prosecutor—a woman a few years Helen's junior—shot him a cold glance before turning to coach Helen's relatives.

She thought he was guilty. They all did. He had not spoken with his wife's family after her death.

The prosecution's case may have been circumstantial, but it was compelling. They put Detective Kelly on the stand first:

No forcible entry was found. From the beginning of the investigation, it did not appear to be a break-in. Nothing was missing.

The forensics technician: *The defendant's prints were found on the neck*

—the soft, delicate skin of Helen's neck; he had brushed the pearl-strand of bruises there—

the gun, bullets, and lamp. No sets were found other than the deceased's.

The jury listened impassively as the 911 recording was played.

Did I hear you right? Your attacker is still in the house? Ma'am?

Helen's barely audible voice, the whisper of a ghost: *He's trying to kill me . . .*

911: *Will you repeat that, please?*

A pause. The sound of the receiver hitting the carpet.

Richard . . . He's trying to kill me . . .

Kimble lowered his face into his hands. Through his fingers, he saw some of the jury lean over to make notes.

Charles Nichols took the stand. Of all Kimble's friends, only Kath Wahlund and Charlie Nichols seemed to sincerely believe in his innocence. Both came to see him in jail, both offered to serve as character witnesses, but Gutherie was interested only in

Nichols. Wahlund, he said, was a little too opinionated, a little too weird to be deemed credible by the jury. Most damning of all, she would not abandon her leather jacket and T-shirt in favor of a navy wool suit.

Nichols did his best.

And then the prosecutor got hold of him. She strode forward, rested a palm on the stand, and turned sideways so the jury could better see the performance. Without moving any closer, she somehow managed to get in Nichols's face.

Her voice was flat, ringing: *Dr. Nichols. You are aware that Richard Kimble was the only beneficiary of Helen Kimble's estate. Twelve million dollars roughly.*

Nichols registered the implication but was unruffled by it. He faced the jury and said with absolute conviction, "I was aware of that. The money meant nothing to him."

Kimble shot him a look of pure gratitude.

The prosecutor seemed unconvinced. She turned on her heel and began to walk, arms folded, toward the jury—away from Nichols. Away from the truth.

Yet in your presence, Richard Kimble once said that if he had Helen's money, he could find plenty of uses. Did he not?

And she stopped, peered back at Nichols, and held him in her unrelenting gaze.

Nichols wavered. "We were talking about—"

About funding medical research. What twelve million dollars could do.

Yes or no?

"If I could just explain—"

The defendant will please answer the question.

Nichols sighed and slumped, defeated, in the chair. The prosecutor smiled, victorious.

No more questions, Your Honor.

The coroner came next. He was a quiet, older man, whose soft, matter-of-fact tone and clinical terms painted a heartrending picture.

The wound to the head caused a massive hemorrhage to the brain. It took from five to seven minutes for her to die . . .

A woman on the jury shuddered, and shot Kimble a look of infinite loathing. He turned away.

When at last they let him take the stand, Kimble spoke simply, haltingly, of the events leading up to Helen's death. He had to stop several times to get hold of himself. When he finished, he looked up to see Gutherie's eyes ashine with hope for the first time; in the jury box, two members reached for tissues and wiped their eyes.

Gutherie nodded approvingly and returned to his seat.

The prosecutor rose and approached slowly, deliberately, like a house cat stalking an unwary bird. Her tone was neutral at first.

How tall was this man, Dr. Kimble?

He blinked as he tried to reach back into memory. "I can't be sure. We were mostly on the floor, fighting. I couldn't—"

Did that fight cause the scratches on your face and arms?

"No. As I explained—"

And how did this man enter your house?

"I don't know—"

And you probably don't know why your wife told the emergency operator you *were her attacker?*

Kimble started to rise from the stand; the judge waved for him to retake his seat. He sat, reluctantly. "She *didn't*—"

The prosecutor smirked. Her voice rose as the questions came fast, faster, faster . . .

Your name is *Richard, isn't it? Your gun* is *a thirty-eight, isn't it? Your prints* were *on the gun, the bullets, the lamp, her neck, weren't they?*

"Look . . ."

Weren't they?

Kimble bowed his head.

Disbelief sustained him. It was simply too horrible to be happening, too insane, too unthinkable, too unjust. He knew the verdict before the jury foreman read it, yet could not absorb it, could not comprehend it as fact. The only reality came to him at night in dreams, in the form of Helen, dying and dead in his arms. In the face of her murderer. Reason said he would never be found, but Kimble had long ago abandoned reason.

It did not matter if he was trapped behind bars and could not find her killer. He would; there was simply no longer any other reason to live.

The guilty verdict came with the first hard frost. On the day Judge Bennett read the sentence, a light snow dusted the city.

Kimble sat in the courtroom beside Gutherie and did not flinch, did not move. A bailiff had to pull him to his feet when the judge said, *Will the defendant please rise . . .*

After careful and studied review of all evidence presented during each phase of this proceeding, and because aggravated circumstances, detailed at length, were *present the night of January twentieth, it is the decision of this court that you be remanded to Menard State Penitentiary, where you will await the penalty of death by lethal injection from the State of Illinois.*

Around him, the sentence shock-waved through the courtroom. A thousand voices began speaking at once; reporters pushed their way to the rear exits as people rose and began scuffling in the aisles. At the prosecution's table, the attorneys shared a look of grim triumph.

Beside him, Gutherie whispered in his ear: "I'm sorry . . ."

But Kimble did not react, did not hear him. He heard only Bennett's words, echoing in his mind. Nor did he notice any of the surrounding commotion; he saw only Helen, and the face of the one-armed man.

And then those visions faded into white swirling nothingness, and he stared straight ahead, wooden, immobile. Snowblind.

3

The old bus coughed as it rolled away from Cook County Jail carrying four prisoners, recently sentenced and bound for Menard State Penitentiary. Kimble leaned against the rumbling metal flank and tried to ignore the stink of diesel and the dull, hostile stares of the three prisoners beside him and the two guards on the other side of the wire mesh cage.

It was night. Shotgun bouncing on his knee, the older of the two guards drowsed, chin sinking to his flat-padded chest, while the younger lit a cigarette and blew the smoke into the cage.

The largest and most dangerous looking of the prisoners growled, "Do that again and I'll make you eat it."

The young guard sneered to show he was not

39

afraid. "Shut your yap, Copeland!" But he blew no more smoke in the prisoners' direction.

Kimble closed his eyes. For the thousandth time since hearing the verdict, he set his mind to work on a solution: He would have to find another attorney, one who believed in his innocence, one who would put his heart into the appeal. One who would hire a private investigator, this time a good one, one who would listen and believe and make an honest effort to track down the one-armed man.

That was all that mattered: finding Helen's killer. Punishing him for hurting her, making sure he could never hurt anyone else again. Everything else was irrelevant. The only thing that mattered was Helen.

The bus labored on for what must have been hours. Despite the ache in his cuffed wrists and chained ankles, despite the cold in the unheated bus, Kimble slept, lulled by the rhythmic motion, and fell into his nightly dream of Helen. Walter Gutherie was there this time, and kept saying he was sorry.

"Hey."

Kimble opened his eyes. A good deal of time had passed, and one of the prisoners, a lean, hard-bitten man with swift, intelligent eyes, had risen and stood beside the wire mesh talking to the younger guard.

"Illinois penal regulations require a meal for transport rides of four hours or more," the prisoner was saying.

The younger guard rolled his eyes and released a grunt that could only be interpreted to mean: *Fucking jailhouse lawyer.* He glanced at his watch, then prodded the snoring older guard with his foot. "Jack! Feedin' time."

Jack came to with a snort, instinctively clutching his shotgun, then relaxed and released a high-pitched yawn. He rose, unhooking the key ring from his belt, and ambled over to the cage while the other guard stowed his weapon in a metal locker. There came the tinkle of metal while Jack fiddled with the lock, then a click, and a loud, wheedling creak as the door swung open.

Kimble stirred and stamped his feet, chains clanking as he tried to get warm, tried to get the blood pumping again. To his left, the prisoner named Copeland leaned forward, cuffed hands and ankles forming a diver's "V," and shook his head between his knees as if trying to rid it of mental cobwebs. Something slid from his shirt and clattered on the scarred steel floor. The sound was hidden by the clinking of Copeland's handcuffs and chains, but Kimble heard, and got an eyeful: it was a plastic shank, the edge sharpened to razor fineness.

Kimble froze. The young guard stepped inside and cautiously reached out to offer a cold, petrified sandwich to the jailhouse lawyer. Kimble glanced back at Copeland, who gracefully palmed the shank despite the cuffs. The burly man leaned closer, emanating the odor of well-aged sweat, and whispered in Kimble's ear.

"Breathe, and you're first."

At the open cage door, old Jack watched with wandering attention, his shotgun propped carelessly against his protruding gut. The young guard gave the second prisoner a sandwich, then reached Kimble and proffered him one; Kimble kept his gaze low and didn't budge.

"Suit yourself." The guard thrust the sandwich at Copeland. The prisoner reached for it and fumbled, unable to recover swiftly because of the handcuffs; the guard swore softly as the sandwich tumbled to the filthy floor. Suddenly helpful, Copeland leaned down to retrieve it. Kimble's heart began to pound with nauseating speed. If he spoke too soon, both he and the guard would be dead.

Up by the cage door, Jack yawned.

"Look out!" Kimble shouted.

Copeland jackknifed up, hands clasped as if in prayer, and drove the shank into the young guard's torso, just beneath the rib cage.

At the same instant, the prisoner on Kimble's right went for the guard's holster. As the pistol slid out, the guard, weaving but still on his feet, got a hand on it. It fired, gouging the steel floor.

The sound galvanized old Jack. He chambered his shotgun, jammed a key into the lock, and dashed into the cage. Kimble hit the floor just as the jailhouse lawyer broadsided the old guard. The shotgun discharged with an explosive, ear-scalding crack, and the old bus gave a lurch, causing the cage door to slam behind them, then increased speed. Kimble raised his face to peer at the front of the vehicle. The pellets had torn a gaping, bloody hole in the back of the driver, who sagged forward and down, putting dead weight on the gas pedal.

The accelerating bus careened off the road. Kimble stayed down, wanting to crawl toward the front to help the driver, but the chains and the free-for-all made progress difficult. Nearby, the young guard wrested the gun from the prisoner on Kimble's right and fired, killing him. Insanely fearless, Copeland hurled himself at the guard and grappled with him for the gun.

A few steps away, old Jack whipped the jailhouse lawyer with the shotgun butt, then flipped the gun in a surprisingly graceful move and pumped a lethal round into the man's chest.

The floor beneath Kimble bucked as the bus, rattling as though it might fly apart, lurched over uneven ground. He managed to pull himself a few inches forward, toward the cage door.

In the meantime, Jack reloaded as Copeland dropped down behind a bouncing seat. The old man jammed the shotgun barrel underneath the seat and pulled the trigger just as the bus struck a pothole. The pellets tore through the seat at an upward angle, missing their target.

Abruptly, Kimble was hurled up and to the right as the bus rolled onto its side, slamming him against legs, torsos, seats, the interior wall of the cage. The impact knocked the wind from him, bruised his shoulders and back.

Still the ride was not over—he sensed forward movement, accompanied by the serpentine groan of metal sliding across gravel. The vehicle filled with a choking cloud of dust.

Then finally all movement, all sound ceased. The engine sputtered and died. Kimble lay flat on his back and struggled to catch his breath, at last sucking in a lungful of dust. He coughed as he pushed himself up to a crouching position.

And found himself staring eye to shotgun barrel with old Jack, who had gone to retrieve his key ring and call to the apparently dead driver on the other side of the cage door, and been startled by the noise. There was a wildness in the old man's eye, left over from the struggle; for a long beat, Kimble thought the guard would shoot him.

He stared back at the man but did not resist, did not utter a single word of discouragement. At that moment he honestly did not care whether Jack shot him or not, except for regretting that Helen's killer would never be found. He only sighed, and in that weary, resigned sound Jack heard something that kept him from squeezing the trigger.

And then the old man's attention was stolen by another sound, this one a moan of pain. He swiveled his head; Kimble followed his gaze, and saw the young guard lying against the wire mesh, clutching his wounded gut. Blood seeped between his fingers.

The older guard jerked his head at Kimble. "You. You're a doctor. C'mere."

Kimble crab-walked over to the injured man. The young guard's shirt was soaked with blood; he was already looking shocky, and starting to lose consciousness. The location of the wound—just below the right rib cage—indicated damage to the spleen. If he got to an emergency room in time, he would make it. If not . . .

The older man had located a dust-covered medical kit; he thrust it at Kimble. "Do somethin'."

In reply, Kimble stared down at his handcuffs, then back up at the guard. Old Jack sighed, dug out his key ring, and unlocked Kimble's cuffs. Kimble rubbed his wrists gratefully, wincing at the pins-and-needles sensation of life coming back to his hands. He snapped open the medical kit—the rusted hinges creaked—and peered into it.

Ransacked. Empty, except for a few yellowing Band-Aids. Kimble immediately turned his attention back to his patient, leaning close to examine the wound. Definitely a lacerated spleen; judging from the copious bleeding, possible ruptured splenic artery. Without looking up, he turned his head toward old Jack, who hovered anxiously. "He isn't going to make it unless he gets to a hospital. Fast."

"Try," Jack ordered, in a tone that allowed no argument.

Kimble started looking around for something to use as a bandage. As he did, a delicate tremor ran through the bus. Jack looked about nervously, but Kimble kept his attention focused on the emergency. He slipped the medical kit under the man's feet. Jack pulled a shirt off one of the dead prisoners, folded it, and handed it to Kimble, who pressed it hard against the gaping wound. The younger man groaned in pain, but Kimble did not ease the pressure.

The bus shivered again, this time harder. Kimble touched a free hand to the wall, and felt a growing vibration, a rumble like an earthquake gaining strength. "Just where the hell are we?"

The old guard knelt down and crawled toward a shattered barred window. What he saw made him bolt to his feet, striking his head against the bus's side, which was now the ceiling.

"Oh, *shit . . .*"

Kimble leaned forward, craned his neck, and saw—and felt a surge of pure adrenaline.

The bus lay across a railroad track. In the distance, a bend grew bright in the light of an oncoming train.

Jack scrambled for the cage door and shook it vainly, hysterically.

"It's locked!" Kimble shouted. "Where are your keys?"

The old man gaped down at his empty belt, then over at Kimble in panicked bewilderment. Kimble scanned the bus in desperation, saw that the shaken guard had thoughtlessly left them on the floor beside his wounded companion. He swiped them up and pitched them to Jack.

Train light filled the vibrating bus, casting moving patchwork shadows across their faces. Kimble gathered the injured man under the arms and dragged him to the front, where the key ring tinkled in Jack's inept, trembling hands.

"Which one?" Kimble screamed, harshly, to bring him out of it. He propped the wounded man against a metal panel and pointed to what he thought was the correct key. "This? This one?"

Jack nodded tremulously. Kimble tore the ring from him and jabbed the key in the lock; it turned with a joyous *click*. Kimble kicked the door open and slipped a shoulder under the wounded man's armpit. He turned to Jack.

"Help me get him—"

The old man did not stop to listen. He knocked Kimble down, climbed over his back, trampling him, and wriggled out through the shattered windshield. Kimble cried out in outrage and pushed himself up to see the injured guard had regained consciousness and was looking at him with wide-eyed fright.

Kimble stared back. The bus was shaking so badly now his teeth rattled; the light brightened painfully with each passing second. If he stayed too long to help—

(Did it matter? Did it really matter whether he lived or died?

In answer, the image of Helen's killer flashed before his eyes.)

And then he heard the whistle and the shriek of the brakes. He went on pure instinct and seized the man. Together they pushed through the windshield into the dazzling light, and somehow he managed to fling the wounded man clear of the tracks onto soft ground.

He leaped, coming down hard on chained ankles, and rolled before he could regain his feet. Running was impossible; the chains would not permit it. He managed a dozen mincing half steps before the train slammed into the bus.

With the shriek and groan of rending steel, it tore the bus in half, spit out spinning shreds of metal. Shrapnel stung Kimble's thigh. He clutched it, gritting his teeth at the pain, but he did not permit himself to stop, did not dare slow his frantic, crippled pace.

Amazingly, the train's forward momentum slowed but did not stop. Kimble heard rather than saw it, just as he heard the shuddering explosion that vibrated in the ground under his shackled feet. At the soft, breathy, ominous *whoosh*, he glanced over his shoulder and saw flames streaming down the sides of the train. Incandescent red-orange against the backdrop of night, the fire illuminated the railroad crossing like daylight, revealing the injured guard lying safely on the opposite bank.

All this Kimble saw in a millisecond, and as he continued to look, never slowing, there was another eardrum-shattering squeal of metal on metal as the flaming locomotive veered off the tracks—away from the guard, directly toward Kimble.

His jaw dropped. He released a barely audible cry as he turned away and began flailing, arms moving frenetically, legs and feet working triple time against the impossible restriction of the chains.

(And in the midst of the instinctual struggle to survive, the part of his mind not overwhelmed by panic asked, *Why? Why struggle?*

Again, the answer came in the face of Helen's killer, the face of the one-armed man.)

Not daring to look at the fiery giant pursuing him, he ran, clutching at the air in front of him as if to pull himself forward with his arms. He could hear the train roaring deafeningly close behind him, could feel its approaching heat.

Abruptly the ground rose under his feet like the

swell of a wave, like a sudden birth of a mountain. Kimble staggered, almost lost his footing, somehow kept going.

Brakes screaming, the train came close, closer; its heat singed the hairs on the back of Kimble's neck, reddened his exposed skin. He clawed the air, lungs and legs burning with effort, at once overwhelmed by an aching desire to live, to be free, to find Helen's killer.

The cry of the brakes and the train's momentum became muffled, then faded altogether. The moving earth stilled. There was no sound save that of the hiss and crackle of flame. Kimble turned and saw, only yards away, the train burrowed into the ground. He looked down, and saw himself standing on a five-foot-high upheaval of earth.

His knees went rubbery then and he might have fallen, but instead a gust of black smoke engulfed him and he coughed, raising a hand to his mouth. A soft tinkle of metal drew his eye, and he looked to see the key ring, still clutched in his hand.

He made his way into a copse of trees and sat, searching by the light of the fire for the key that would loose his manacles and make him a free man. He was on his fifth try when a hand reached down and yanked the key ring from his grasp.

"Give me that," Copeland snarled. The light from the burning train painted his face with a reddish glow, broken by long, dark stripes of shadow from the trees. Kimble watched as Copeland bent down and quickly unlocked his own chains and cuffs.

"You listen to me," Copeland said, in a tone that

conveyed both threat and promise. "I don't give a damn which way you go—just don't follow me."

Kimble gave a wide-eyed nod; he had no inclination to do so. Copeland threw the keys down, and Kimble retrieved them, picked out the two Copeland had used, and unlocked his leg irons as the other man disappeared into the darkness.

He slipped the chains off with a sense of almost-tearful gratitude, and stood, drawing in a breath at his newfound lightness and agility. By moon- and fire-light, he ran. The night was cold; clumps of frosted dead grass crunched beneath his shoes. But the sky was clear and starry, and there was no threat of snow.

Deputy U.S. Marshal Samuel Gerard stepped from the plain-wrap G sedan and took a good look at the circus. Spotlights revealed fire engines hosing down the charred smoldering train, its nose buried in a bank of earth where it had derailed; overhead, choppers circled billowing smoke while rescuers used the jaws-of-life to pry open the mangled Illinois Department of Corrections bus. The bus had been sheared in half, both halves flattened. No one inside could have survived the impact. No one at all.

Gerard looked at the scene and instinctively didn't like it. Didn't like it at all. He could smell sloppiness miles away.

He moved toward the circus, joining the four who had stepped from the G car parked in front of his: the scrub-faced G-5, Newman, and Marshals Biggs, Renfro, Poole. They walked along the service road above the crash site, staring at the accordioned railcars below.

Biggs spotted something in the smoking wreckage and said, "Point of impact."

He veered off. Gerard called after him.

"Biggs. Your turn to baby-sit Newman."

Biggs looked with undisguised scorn over his shoulder at the young greenhorn G-5. "Shit . . ." He jerked his head reluctantly at Newman. "Come on."

Flushing, Newman followed Biggs down to the crash site. Renfro, a skinny rooster of a man, and Poole, a black woman with a gaze that could freeze lava, followed Gerard. They headed into a group of news reporters. Gerard pushed his way through, and a state trooper moved into his path, blocking him from the accident scene.

Gerard flashed his badge. The trooper stepped aside, abruptly cooperative.

"Who's in charge?" Gerard asked. In the periphery of his vision, he saw Renfro and Poole share a look: *Whoever it is, he won't be for long . . .* Gerard did not mind. In fact, it secretly pleased him.

"Sheriff Rollins." The trooper pointed. "Just follow the lights . . ."

Gerard squinted in the direction of the gesture. Atop a nearby knoll, television lights shone brilliantly, blindingly, obliterating those atop it from view. He shook his head in disgust and started up.

Renfro and Poole followed, their lips pursing as they repressed knowing smirks.

The glare receded as Gerard ascended the hill and passed the television lights, which were focused on the man seated near a tall evergreen. He was sixtyish, gray-haired, and thick-waisted, his face smudged with soot, his eyes slightly wide with the bright, mindless shock Gerard saw so often in his work. Beneath the space blanket draped over his shoulders, the man wore a torn Department of Corrections uniform. He was attended solicitously by paramedics, a remote news crew, and a thirtyish sheriff who was clearly basking in the excitement.

The old man was speaking, and Gerard paused at the edge of the crowd to listen.

". . . train was bearin' down on us, fast. I don't know how—it's still kinda hazy—but I grabbed him and pushed him out of the bus."

"You coulda both been killed," the sheriff said, speaking clearly for the reporters' behalf, angling himself so the camera got a full profile. Gerard's lips tightened in a small, grim line.

The old man nodded, thoughtful. "I know. But hell, he's my partner. Woulda done the same for me."

The reporters were eating it up. Gerard chose that moment to interrupt; he moved forward, displaying his badge.

"Excuse me. Sheriff Rollins? Deputy U.S. Marshal Samuel Gerard."

Annoyed, the sheriff jerked his head to glare at the interloper. "I'll be with you in a minute."

The scope of the lights broadened to include Gerard. He glared with undisguised disdain at the cameraman, but closed his mouth and said nothing more, showing no sign of offense, of the cold hate he felt for the arrogant asshole sheriff. He did not say that it was because of incompetents like Rollins that innocent people died. Instead, he watched without comment as the sheriff opened a file and spread fax photos of four prisoners in front of the old man.

"For the record," Rollins said, pointing. "These three dead. And this one, Kimble . . ."

Gerard caught a glimpse and moved closer, intrigued by the photograph in the file. Not your typical booking shot, not your typical criminal. This guy wore a tuxedo shirt and black tie—definitely white collar, definitely loaded. Gerard glanced down at the two shredded metal pancakes that remained of the prisoner transport bus, at the blackened train, then back at the photo. This Kimble had fallen from cushy circumstances; he looked like a spoiled rich kid, not the sort to have the survival instincts to make it out of that smoldering wreckage alive.

The old man hesitated, raised a filthy hand to his mouth. "Well, everything happened so fast . . ." He chewed his bottom lip a few seconds, then came to a decision and shook his head. "Huh uh. Don't think he made it."

Sheriff Rollins looked down at the charred ruins, then filed Kimble's photograph along with the others and closed the file.

"You get some rest." He smiled and patted the old man on the shoulder, then rose and moved over to Gerard. "Looks like you came a long way for nothing," Rollins said, with infuriating smugness. "My men have already done a thorough search from point of impact and found nothing."

Conscious of the media, Gerard stared back with a mild expression of distaste while hating Rollins with a vehemence that would have terrified the young man had he known. He could not bear sloppy work, could not bear assumptions; he had seen the toll it took in lives.

He gazed at Sheriff Rollins and said patiently, "With all due respect, may I suggest checkpoints starting at a fifteen-mile radius on I-Fifty-seven, I-Twenty-four, Route Thirteen east of—"

"Whoa, whoa, whoa . . ." Rollins scowled, pudgy young face screwing into an expression of irritation; he waved his hands, palms out, at Gerard. "For *what*? Prisoners are all dead. The only thing checkpoints will do is get a lot of good people out here frantic and flood my office with calls."

Gerard moved in. He stepped toe-to-toe with Rollins and locked him in a stony gaze. The younger man recoiled, for the first time seeming to sense the hatred emanating from Gerard like body heat.

"Well, shit, Sheriff," Gerard said softly, with mocking regret. "I'd hate for that to happen . . . so I'll just be taking over the investigation." He knew, without looking, that behind him Poole and Renfro smiled.

Rollins lifted his formless chin in a pale effort at defiance. "On whose authority?"

Gerard did not quite smile; he had been waiting some time for the opportunity to answer that particular question. "By authority of the Governor of the State of Illinois and the office of the United States Marshal, Fifth District Northern Illinois . . ."

As he spoke, Poole produced the state and federal authorizations from her pocket and displayed them to the young sheriff.

Rollins wilted. He lowered his voice so the reporters could not hear as he said, "Okay. You want jurisdiction over this mess, you got it." He jerked his head toward his assistants and yelled, "Shut it down! Wyatt Earp is here to mop up for us." He thrust the file of prisoner photos at the marshal's chest as he strode past.

At the same moment, Biggs was moving toward them, a pair of mud-encrusted leg irons in his hands. Rumpled sleeves and pantlegs coated with mud, Newman staggered behind him. Biggs, of course, was spotless.

At the sight of the empty manacles, Rollins and his deputies pulled up and wheeled about. Gerard gave them a coldly triumphant look as he sidled up to the old man, and gestured for the press to step back.

"Please, ladies and gentlemen, step back and give this poor man some room."

Everyone backed off. With Poole and Renfro beside him, Gerard knelt in front of the old man. "Always an interesting thing when we find leg irons and no legs in them . . . Who held the keys, sir?"

The guard blinked up at him. "Uh . . . me."

"Would you be so kind as to show them to me, sir?" Gerard held out his hand, palm up, expectantly.

The guard fumbled at his belt, then his pockets. He eyed the press nervously.

"Second chance," Gerard said. He gestured, and

Poole reopened the folder full of photos, held it so the guard could see. "Want to start over?"

The old man averted his eyes, unable to meet Gerard's uncompromising stare. He pored over the photographs again, then timidly pointed at the one labeled "Dr. Richard Kimble." "He mighta got out."

"Thank you," Gerard said sincerely.

"What the hell is this?" Rollins demanded. "A minute ago, you tell me he's part of the wreckage! Now you're telling *him*—"

Gerard ignored him. "Renfro—take that bus apart. Poole—set up operations here." He started moving downtrack, speaking as he went to the small army of Illinois State troopers and press that followed. "Ladies and gentlemen . . . our fugitive's been on the run for ninety minutes. Average foot speed over uneven ground—barring injury—is approximately four miles an hour, giving us a radius of six miles. I want a hard-target search of any residence, gas station, farmhouse, henhouse, doghouse, and outhouse in that area. Checkpoints go up at fifteen miles."

He pulled up abruptly and squinted, scowling, into the television lights, and said to the media, "You got that? Good." He gestured at the lights. "Now turn these damned things off and get out of our way."

Kimble ran lightly, following the train tracks as they wound through dark forest. He ran until the painful throbbing in his thigh demanded attention, until he could no longer ignore the blood that trickled into his shoe. He paused to duck under the cover of a tree and leaned against the rough, sweet-smelling pine trunk. In the darkness, he could see little, but he probed the outline of the laceration gently with his fingers. The shrapnel had gouged a jagged hole, but fortunately there seemed to be no bits of metal embedded in his flesh. Even so, the wound was deep and wide, requiring stitches. Otherwise, there was no doubt it would become infected—and although the bleeding wasn't immediately life threatening, he had to do something about it before he became weak.

Kimble looked up. The tracks seemed to lead straight toward the not-too-distant glow of city lights; if he could get to a town, he could find a hospital.

Hope alternated with despair. There was a chance, if the police were sloppy, they would assume, looking at the wreckage, that he was dead—at least until the young guard he'd rescued recovered enough to talk. That would give him several hours, time to make it to a hospital, time to get what he needed to take care of his wound.

Time to recover and make it back to Chicago and track down Helen's killer.

But if the old guard, Jack, had seen him escape . . . If the young guard made a miraculous recovery . . . If they captured Copeland and made him talk . . . If they combed the area and found the leg irons too soon . . .

Then they would set up roadblocks, and they would have cops waiting for him at every hospital in the area. If they were smart.

Kimble forced himself to stop thinking. All those things made no difference. He had to try to disinfect and suture the wound; otherwise he would be dead from septicemia before he ever made it to Chicago. If there were cops at the hospital, he'd simply have to figure out a way to get around them. If he could just figure out how to get his hands on a change of clothes . . .

He pushed against the bark and began moving again, toward the beckoning glow.

4

Thirty minutes later, he had made his way to civilization, and the wood's edge. On the same side of a two-lane highway sat a junkyard, and beside it a lone street lamp, which shone down upon a Department of Transportation sign:

HOSPITAL
EMERGENCY
½ MI
←

Kimble approached the junkyard cautiously, fearful of an encounter, but the place seemed deserted. He moved toward some of the rusted-out cars, hoping vainly to find one that still worked, when a rumble came down the highway. Kimble scurried behind a tree, peering between the branches as a tow truck, with a wrecked car on its hook, pulled up to the junkyard gate. He stole closer as the portly balding driver climbed out, tossed a wadded-up pair of coveralls onto the front seat, slammed the door, and shuffled up to the gate.

Kimble seized his opportunity. While the driver's back was turned, he slipped a hand inside the open window of the truck and swiped the coveralls.

He almost didn't make it. The driver stepped up to the gate, hesitated, and immediately turned and headed back for the truck. Kimble froze, crouching, on the other side, while the man opened the driver's-side door and grabbed a bagged lunch off the seat. Through some miracle of inattention, he failed to notice the missing coveralls.

Kimble released a slow, shaking breath, waited for the man to enter the gate, then fled back into the woods to change. No point in stealing the tow truck; the theft would be detected and reported too quickly, alerting his pursuers.

As he buried his bloody prison clothes in the dirt, then pulled on the stolen coveralls, Kimble could not help reflecting on the irony that his wrongful conviction had forced him to commit his very first crime.

Poole had erected a makeshift headquarters in a tent near the crash site, with power and phone lines pulled down from those running alongside the tracks. Gerard sat at a card table covered with maps—all of them decorated with red marks and circles.

But at that moment, Gerard was not looking at the maps; he was studying the faxed booking photo of Richard Kimble.

The bus had been going to Menard—not a nice place. Menard was where they sent the tough guys, the ones convicted of violent crimes. Also the ones sitting on death row. Whatever Kimble had done, it had not been pretty. Most likely someone had died.

Yet the eyes . . . the eyes were not right. Gerard had seen thousands, hundreds of thousands, of booking photos in his day. He knew the look in a killer's eyes: the dull resentment, the hint of crazed amusement, the defiance, and sometimes—worst of all—the indifference.

Kimble's eyes were not like that at all. There was some anger in them, yes, some hostility, but these did not dominate. There was something far more disturbing in them, something Sam Gerard at first did not want to identify—but he forced himself, because there was nothing more important to Gerard than the truth. Kimble's eyes bespoke horror, bespoke an emotion so powerful that it took some time before Gerard, used to dealing with hardened cops and hardened criminals, was able to identify it, before he was able to find the right word.

Grief.

Crime of passion, then? Committed in a moment of fury, then regretted?

If so, he should have gotten off a lot easier than Menard.

At the other end of the tent, Poole listened to her radio, then called to Gerard. "Blood trail found. Two miles southwest."

"Type it and match it against all four prisoners," Gerard ordered without having to think. Poole nodded, moved toward a phone. Gerard turned toward Renfro. "Renfro, get an I.D. fax on Kimble to every local hospital." He paused. "Newman!"

"Yes, sir." Newman snapped to attention eagerly; he had been listening and was ready to do his part.

Inwardly, Gerard smiled an evil smile, but kept his expression stony. He and his staff had spent the past week taking delight in tormenting the new recruit; the hazing was more enjoyable than usual because Newman was so eminently tormentable.

"I need some coffee."

Newman sagged, deflated, as he moved to obey.

Gerard went back to staring at Kimble's photograph.

Who did you kill, Dr. Richard Kimble? And why?

Whoever it was, Gerard would see to it he did not have the chance again. Ever.

He glanced up as a shout came up from the crash site, from one of the rescue workers.

"Hey! This one's alive!"

Kimble reached the hospital at dawn. There was no sign of the police in the parking lot, and he spied his opportunity early on: a truck had backed up to the delivery entrance, and the driver and one of the hospital kitchen staff were unloading pallets of institutional canned goods.

Kimble kept his head down and angled himself behind one of the stacked pallets so that the workers never saw him as they entered. Once inside, he slipped away down a different hallway.

His luck continued. The first minor-procedures room he found was empty. He shut the door behind him and rifled through cabinets until he found what he needed: a suture set, forceps, Lidocaine, ampicillin and syringe, antibacterial wash, bandages—even a white lab coat, which was good because a small amount of blood had seeped onto the thigh of the coveralls. He elbowed into the lab coat and crammed the supplies into the coveralls, then cleaned the wound, sutured himself up, injected himself with the ampicillin, then slipped back into the hall.

There was still the problem of clothing, food, money—and the beard.

He made his way onto a patients' floor and started reading charts by the doors until he found a male of appropriate height and weight, one who had been prescribed sedation; he stole into the room.

Bingo. An intubated man about Kimble's size lay asleep, mouth open. Kimble quietly pulled the door closed, then moved over to the man.

"Can you hear me, sir?"

No reply. Kimble went silently over to the closet and slipped the man's clothes from their hangers. Change jingled in the pants pocket. Kimble pulled out a wad of one-dollar bills, considered leaving the money—then stuffed them back into the pocket. He would need money if he was to survive. Guiltily, he lifted a pair of prescription reading glasses from the bedside table and hoped that the man had an extra pair.

Crime number two.

Kimble stepped out of the dirty coveralls and into the clean street clothes. Nearby, an untouched breakfast rested on the tray table; he helped himself to a piece of toast and wolfed it down.

Passing by the open door to the tiny bathroom, he passed a mirror and caught sight of himself: disheveled, dirty-faced, with an unkempt silver-streaked beard. His eyes wandered to the shaving kit on the sink and he paused, remembering the photograph they had taken at the police station the night of Helen's death.

He was halfway through when the duty nurse entered; he held his breath and hid behind the door in the bathroom. She never noticed, not even when she came into the bathroom to fill the man's pitcher from the sink.

He finally left the man's room clean-shaven and bespectacled, with the white lab smock over street clothes. Heading down the corridor, he began to feel a sense of exhilaration: he was going to make it. All he had to do was walk out the front, then call Walter Gutherie and—

He stopped. At the front-desk phone, only feet from Kimble, only yards away from the main exit and freedom, a uniformed highway patrolman was watching a fax come over the machine.

Kimble did a graceful one-eighty. The trooper looked up and started moving toward him.

" 'Scuse me, Doc?"

Kimble faced him but continued backing toward the E.R. doors, fighting the impulse to run.

"Don't know if you heard or not," the trooper said, "but we're looking for an escaped prisoner from that bus and train wreck a couple hours ago. Thought he might show up here if he was hurt."

Kimble forced an interested expression. "What's he look like?"

The trooper glanced down at the fax, and Kimble suddenly felt a tiny trickle on his cheek. He touched a finger to it; the tip came away bloody. He wiped it quickly with his hand as the trooper read from the fax sheet.

"Approximately six one, one-eighty pounds, brown hair, brown eyes, and graying beard." The trooper looked up. "Seen anyone that fits that description?"

"Every time I look in the mirror, but without the beard," Kimble said.

The trooper laughed.

"Excuse me." Kimble pushed through the swinging doors to the E.R. The trooper did not follow, and no one else stopped him, no one asked questions; he looked like the doctor that he was, on his way to an emergency. He kept straight on, passing out of the building onto the E.R. ramp, behind a parked ambulance.

The rear doors of the ambulance crashed open in front of him, blocking his path. He drew back, startled, as under his nose paramedics wheeled a patient on a gurney. The lead wheels stuck on the ramp. Kimble leaned down and cleared them.

"Here."

"Thanks, Doc," one of them said. "We had to dig him out from under a train."

The gurney slid forward, and he found himself staring into the eyes of the young guard, the man whose life he had saved. The medics had done their job. The color had come back to his face, and he seemed somewhat responsive.

Too responsive. His half-open eyes blinked, narrowed, then opened wide. His mouth was covered by a portable oxygen mask, but he pushed it weakly away. "It's him . . . it's Kim—"

Kimble clamped the mask back over his mouth and glanced up at the paramedics. "How is he?"

"Pretty bad off," the first paramedic said. "Broken leg, ribs. Concussion."

"Tell the E.R. doctor he's also got a perforated spleen."

The first paramedic gazed at him in pure awe. As the two of them whisked the gurney into the E.R., Kimble heard one say, "Jesus, how could he tell that from lookin' at his *face*?"

Knees rubbery, Kimble leaned against the ambulance's flank for a few seconds, then climbed into the driver's seat.

The crash site had grown quiet, except for a handful of rescue workers, still sifting through the debris; the circus had moved to the marshals' encampment on the hillside above. Gerard and his lackeys answered ever-ringing phones, hovered over incoming and outgoing faxes, hastened to add information to the big situation board. A steady stream of troopers, bearing nuggets of information, came and went.

At Gerard's elbow, Renfro stripped a fax hot off the machine and held it aloft so Poole, stepping up and squinting at it curiously, could read it too. Gerard caught a glimpse of Kimble's photo alongside a ream of data. He could not see Renfro's expression, but he saw Poole's, her dark forehead creased in puzzlement. Gerard wondered if she saw what he had in Kimble's eyes.

Poole finished reading and declaimed, "Background just came in from Chicago."

Gerard swiveled toward her. "Hit me."

Renfro read in his clear tenor. A whole head taller, and half again as wide, Poole stood beside him. "Richard David Kimble. Vascular surgeon. Convicted of first-degree murder in the killing of his wife. He was headed for Menard to sit on death row."

So, Gerard thought. *It* was *a crime of passion.*

Renfro continued. "Pleaded innocent. Claimed a one-armed man—"

Gerard stopped him. "Let's not retry the case." He rose and stepped out onto the hillside, searching for just the right secluded spot.

Poole and Renfro were familiar with the routine and went with him.

"Priors and accomplices?" Gerard asked, stationing himself in front of a tree.

"None," Renfro replied. "No previous arrests."

On the other side of the tree, Poole discreetly turned her back as Gerard unzipped his fly and relieved himself. "Sealed juvie record?" he asked.

"Nothing," Poole called out. "Total cherry."

"Relatives? Children?"

Renfro answered. "No relatives . . ."

"One child," Poole said, with a curious softness Gerard had never heard in her voice. "A son. Died in a drowning accident three years ago."

Gerard's bear trap of a mind eased open just a bit, enough to allow the monosyllabic thought: *Grief.*

He censored it immediately, and worked to paint a different mental image of this surgeon, who had been on his way to Menard for a reason. "Girlfriends? Ex-wives? Friends? Combinations of the above?"

But Poole did not provide him with the out he sought: a reason to dislike Kimble. "Lots of friends. Doctors. Hospital staff."

Gerard shook, tucked, and zipped. "Start there. Authorize taps. Cover his lawyer first."

Renfro's dark eyes widened with mild shock. "Never get it."

Gerard stepped up to him and lowered his gaze to hold Renfro's. "Bet me."

Renfro graced him with a sheepish half smile and shook his head; he had been working with Gerard long enough to know better.

Gerard gave a single curt nod of satisfaction. "Have Stevens go to Judge Rubin. He'll sign 'em."

The three of them turned as Biggs, breathless and flushed, charged up the hillside. "DeLange Hospital," he gasped, clutching a side stitch. "Wounded guard swears to High Holy he saw Kimble right there in the hallway. Ambulance missing, too."

Gerard returned to the tent and strode up to the map with the swift purposefulness of an arrow seeking its target. "Give me a time," he said to Biggs.

"Oh-nine-thirty. Twenty minutes ago."

Gerard redrew the circle of units so that it no longer spanned a fifty-mile radius. The new circle was smaller, with the hospital at its center. He thought of Kimble, and felt the grim satisfaction of a hangman tightening the noose.

In the speeding ambulance, Kimble was listening to police chatter over the biocom.

The close call and the taste of freedom left him exhilarated. He had a sense of purpose for the first time since Helen's death; it was the only thing that eased his grief. He realized now that he could never go to prison, could not permit his life and Helen's death to fade into meaninglessness.

For Helen's sake, he was determined not to die— not before he found the man who had killed her.

A bored voice crackled over the biocom. "We're waiting up here in Canton. Wondering if you heard anything on this Kimble chase—"

Kimble leaned forward, attentive, braking as three

cars in front of him slowed for a rural railroad crossing.

The police dispatcher came on the radio. "Two-twelve-A, be advised that all discussion on this matter is to be conducted on a tactical frequency—either Channel K or Z. Over."

The frequency went dead. Kimble sighed, then turned his head quickly to read a fast-receding road sign: CANTON, 2 MI.

The cars in front came to a full stop as the railroad crossing signal flashed red; the bars began to slowly drop.

Kimble turned on the siren and gunned the accelerator. The ambulance snaked through the lowering bars over the tracks, and sped off.

Poole hung up the phone and turned toward Gerard. Her usually calm, unruffled tone was a half-octave higher in pitch than normal. "Ambulance just spotted two miles west of Doverville. Heading north of State Road Fifty-three."

Renfro turned toward the map and marked it, adding a large red X alongside those for the crash site and the hospital, and drawing an ever-smaller circle. The noose was growing tighter. He shot a sidewise glance at Gerard. "Running out of map, Sam."

Gerard's lips thinned in a grimly pleased expression. "Just the way we want it." He rose. "Okay, people, let's button up."

He headed toward the waiting helicopter with an odd sense of anticipation. The anticipation he usually felt, that of seeing a criminal stopped from endangering the public, that of seeing justice done.

On instinct, Kimble swung the ambulance around and headed in the opposite direction, south, into Kentucky. He made it over the state line trembling with relief to find no roadblocks waiting there.

The terrain grew luxuriantly green and hilly. The two-lane highway climbed until the ambulance rolled along the top of a crest. Traffic picked up; a rural version of morning rush hour was just beginning. Kimble fumbled through the glove compartment and under the seats for a map, finally finding one when he flipped down the visor. He unfolded it and propped it against the steering wheel.

A few hundred feet below, the Tennessee River reflected morning sun like quicksilver. Rising out of it came the great, curving arches of the Grosvenor Viaduct; in the near distance rose the Barkley Dam.

Kimble headed onto the viaduct and into a long, dimly lit tunnel. He had almost made it to the other side and could see the sunlight when he heard the chopper overhead. It touched down at the mouth of the tunnel, in the dead center of the roadway.

Kimble slammed on the brakes, slinging his arm across the back of the seat and turning to look behind him. Other brakes squealed. Cars fishtailed as horns blared and angry drivers shouted curses.

Behind him, at the tunnel's other entrance, highway patrol cars formed a roadblock. Troopers were already setting down lighted flares.

Stricken, Kimble stared forward again. For a split second, he did not see the additional troopers pull up behind the helicopter, did not see them step out of their vehicles and draw their weapons. He saw only Helen, the side of her head blown away as she struggled to speak.

My head. Richard . . . my . . . hold . . . me . . .

And as she spoke, her face changed, metamorphosed to become that of her killer's.

Her words were drowned out as the P.A. began to blare: *Please remain in your vehicles and lock your doors. Repeat, please remain in your vehicles . . .*

"**G**ot him," Renfro said with relish as he handed his boss a bulletproof vest. As always, he stood beside Poole, the two of them already decked out in Kevlar.

Gerard slipped on the proffered vest and unholstered his pride and joy, a .40-caliber Glock model 22. He felt satisfied at a job professionally done; he also felt oddly disappointed that it had been this easy. For some reason, he had hoped Kimble would give them more of a chase.

At the same time, he felt some relief that it was over. He wanted to take Kimble himself; he prayed the man would let them take him alive. There were a few questions Gerard wanted to ask about those eyes.

He glanced from Poole to Renfro to the tunnel, dark and depthless. "Okay, ladies and gentlemen. Hard part's over."

In truth, he feared the hardest part had just begun.

As they began to walk, Renfro raised his radio to his lips. "We're going in . . ."

*P*lease remain in your vehicle and lock your doors . . .

At mid-tunnel, Kimble slipped from the ambulance into the dank, exhaust-laden air and watched as, against the backdrop of light at the tunnel's mouth, three silhouettes with drawn weapons approached. He dropped to the ground and wriggled beneath the ambulance, hands and knees stung by the icy, trickling water, by the rough surfaces.

Instinct said to lie still, not resist, let them take him. Instinct said to survive at all costs.

But determination and sorrow overruled. He could not go to prison, to meaningless existence, to endless grief. In prison there was no chance of finding Helen's killer; the only hope lay in freedom. He would resist at all costs, gladly risk his life for any chance, no matter how infinitesimal, of escape. If need be, he would die. After all, death was at the end of this dark, cold path anyway.

But lying huddled against the cold, wet asphalt, he saw no option other than death. There was no getting out of the tunnel, past the armed troopers on either side. There were only two ways out, and both of them were blocked. Only two . . .

He stared in the dimness at the rivulets of cold water trickling over the backs of his flattened hands, and with his gaze followed the current to the large iron gate recessed in the asphalt.

Renfro and Poole fanned out to the sides and gave Gerard the middle. He moved deliberately, cautiously, wheeling with gun ready when a stray driver, without enough sense to heed the P.A. warning, got a good look at him and hightailed it back into his car and slammed the door. The sound echoed in the tunnel, quiet except for the droning warning:

Repeat, please remain in your vehicle . . .

Blessedly, the P.A. abruptly ceased. Gerard concentrated on the sounds: his own breathing, his soft, measured steps, the barely audible, distant footfall of Renfro and Poole, the faint gurgle of water.

At mid-tunnel, they caught up to Biggs, who had done a sweep coming from the other end. Biggs's expression showed the same as those of Renfro and Poole: confusion. The three looked again under vehicles, inside them. Gerard closed his eyes and listened with his entire being.

"Where'd he go?" Poole asked at last, exasperated, and Gerard opened his eyes, walked to where the road's shoulder met the tunnel, and pointed to the small, steady stream of water. Accompanied by Poole, he backtracked it until he spotted the grate in the pavement. Loose. Man-sized.

He felt the thrill of challenge; he felt intense irritation. "Biggs!" he snapped. "Renfro! With me."

The grate lifted easily, too easily. The three wriggled down into the storm drain—Renfro first, small and agile, then Gerard, then Biggs, who with his barrel chest almost couldn't make it through; he had to raise his arms over his head and be pulled down. Poole tossed them flashlights.

Below, the tunnel echoed with distant, steady thunder. The water was ankle high, the current strong, the concrete moss-green and slick. Gerard moved gingerly on unsure footing, sweeping his light over the conduit wall, just above the water level, and found the fresh splash patterns that told of Kimble's passing. The three men made their way to a group of forking tunnels. Renfro made a noise and gestured with his light toward one of them: a jacket lay abandoned in the water.

Gerard fingered his radio. "Channel Three."

Biggs and Renfro conformed their radios, and the group split up, with Gerard taking the conduit that lay straight ahead—the path he knew, with a predator's instinct, that Kimble had taken. Gerard was always first to find the escapees, and Poole joked he had the nose of a bloodhound. At slack times, when things got too dull, they would play a game: he would close his eyes, and she would wave everyone's weapons under his nose and say: *Okay, whose is this?* And he would answer, *That's Renfro's.* Or: *That's easy—that's my Glock.* And ninety percent of the time, he would be right. Sometimes they just held their palms in front of his face, in which case he never missed.

He imagined he could smell Kimble now.

The conduit forked again, off to the right, and he probed the downward-sloping tunnel with his light.

He almost passed, but something—Kimble's scent—made him hesitate, and look again. At shoulder level, there were areas where the moss had been scraped away—most likely by human hands.

He lifted the radio, spoke into it. "Got a possible here. Stand by."

He stowed the flashlight in his jacket. Bracing with three limbs, the Glock clutched in his right hand, Gerard eased his way down into the tunnel.

Descent was tricky because of the downward slope and Gerard's smooth-soled shoes. He slipped once, almost going down on one knee, but recovered and inched forward more slowly, pressing harder against the treacherous slime.

A few feet later, he slipped again. The Glock and the radio clattered away, then came to rest with a splash as Gerard careened out of control, arms and legs scrabbling vainly for purchase. He found it at last in the form of an overhead pipe; he snagged it, managed to get his feet and hands braced again. Struggling to maintain balance, he pulled out the flashlight, switched it on, and scanned the murky runoff until he saw the Glock's glistening barrel sticking out from the water's edge. He eased slowly toward it, worrying less about his footing than about nicks and scratches, and whether he would be able to polish them out. It took his full concentration to bend down without sliding forward, one hand bracing him against the slippery wall, one hand reaching forward, carefully, carefully . . .

A strange hand grasped it first. Gerard jerked his

head to stare up into hauntingly familiar eyes, eyes he had begun to brood over during the past twenty-four hours, eyes that belonged to Dr. Richard David Kimble.

5

Gerard locked gazes with his prey.

Kimble's face wore the dark, wild look of the hunted; his expression, as his white-knuckled hand flexed on the pistol, was threatening, intended to inspire fear. This was a dangerous man, Gerard told himself, a very desperate man. An escaped killer. A man sentenced to die for the treacherous crime he had committed.

He was not for a moment afraid. He had not imagined what the faxed booking photo revealed of Kimble's character; he saw the same look in Kimble's eyes now. Kimble would not use the gun.

Gerard coiled, ready to spring at the first opportunity.

"I didn't kill my wife," Kimble said suddenly.

"So you didn't kill your wife," Gerard said. "Not my problem."

Kimble started at a crackle of static. Down-tunnel, Biggs's voice filtered through the half-submerged radio. "Gerard? You there?"

Gerard turned, instinctively following the sound of Biggs's voice—for a second, less than second—and when he looked back, Kimble had vanished.

He reached for his ankle and withdrew a pistol, then propelled himself, half sliding, half running, down the conduit. From a side tunnel, Renfro abruptly appeared; the two almost collided.

"Straight ahead!" Gerard shouted.

Biggs heard the commotion and joined them, and the chase was on.

Kimble stuck the gun in his waistband and careened down the tunnel, following the sound of rushing water until it became a deafening roar that obliterated all other sound, all thought. He skidded around a corner and came to a stop.

The tunnel ended abruptly. Ahead: Light. Noise, a crashing so intense he yearned to shield his ears with his hands. Water surged past his ankles onto the spillway of Barkley Dam and fell in a violent, powerful cascade some hundred feet into a veil of mist below.

The awesome sight evoked terror; he balked.

If he hit the water at a bad angle, he'd be killed on impact—if he didn't drown first when the furious falls pounded him into unconsciousness.

He could not die. For Helen's sake, he could not die.

Footsteps, splashing behind him. Kimble turned to see the man whose gun he had stolen standing behind him, armed this time with a smaller weapon. Another man, shorter, leaner, accompanied him, and crouched, leveling his weapon at Kimble's chest.

"Turn around," the first man ordered, in a voice as hard and emotionless as stone. "Hands over your head. And get down on the ground."

Kimble obediently turned and faced the water.

"Get down on your knees," the man said.

Hearing footsteps behind him, Kimble bent slowly, staring into the falls, and jumped.

Renfro lowered his gun in amazement. "Son of a bitch . . ."

Gerard stood at the tunnel's mouth and felt cool spray on his face as he stared into the rising mists.

He was thinking about Kimble's leap. It was an insane act, the sort of act one might expect from a crazed killer; and he had seen Kimble face-to-face now, seen the wild desperation in the man's eyes. The obsession.

By late afternoon, Gerard's superiors insisted he call off the search because of budget considerations, but he made sure that Kimble's fax photo found its way into every police station and sheriff's office in six surrounding states.

Below the dam and spillway, troopers waded
through the shallows and beat bushes along the banks
as the sun slipped toward the horizon. From shore,
Gerard watched the dredge boat bring the cage up
again and again: empty. Empty. Empty. He felt a curious mixture of disappointment and relief.

The trooper captain stepped up behind Gerard,
who did not turn. "Running out of daylight, Inspector."

Gerard watched as the boat lowered the cage
again. "Lights and generators are coming, Captain."

The trooper adopted a familiar, confidential tone
that Gerard found offensive. "Look, I don't mean to
tell you your job, but maybe one person in a million
could've survived that fall. The guy's fish food."

Gerard looked over his shoulder and directed his
most intensely scathing stare at the captain. "Then
find me the fish that ate him."

He turned back and watched as the dredge, dripping water and tangled in flotsam, emerged again.

Empty. Empty. Empty.

The water pummeled the breath from Kimble's
lungs, crashed against him with the bruising force of
hurled stone. He descended through the falls mindless, deafened, gasping.

When he thought his lungs emptied of air, he
struck the unforgiving surface of the reservoir, and
the last bit of breath was slapped from him.

He fought to the surface, sucking in oxygen as he
was swept away, through the deep to the shallows in

the lower reservoir, where man-made concrete gave way to rushes and grassy riverbank. Downstream where the river curved, he collided into a mass of rushes and driftwood, snagged by an overhanging tree limb. He reached for it, grasped it, tried to pull himself up, but the current was too strong. The branch snapped, and he sailed away, still clutching it.

After a time the current eased, and he emerged dripping onto the bank. He walked for miles along the secluded riverbank, shivering as the wind and feeble winter sun dried his soaked clothes—and smiling grimly when he discovered four soggy one-dollar bills and change in his pocket, and the gun still securely tucked in his waistband. Crimes three and four: resisting arrest, and stealing a weapon. He had not been a criminal when this had begun, but he was rapidly becoming one now. He went to the river's edge, and tossed the gun into the dark water.

He walked until night came, ignoring the ache of his battered body, strengthened by the exhilaration of success, of survival, by the firm belief that he would find the one-armed man. He found privacy and shelter from the wind beneath a railroad trestle; for warmth, he covered himself with cardboard remnants and dead boughs of hemlock, and fell at once into exhausted sleep. Above, a train rumbled.

Kimble did not wake, but the noise made its way into the periphery of his subconscious, and he drifted into an anxious tangle of images: the light of the oncoming train, the sensation of being trapped inside the overturned bus, the wide-eyed look of panic on the young guard's face as he thought Kimble would leave him to die, and again, the same expression on his face as he recognized his rescuer at the hospital.

The images coalesced into a dream. Suddenly Kimble was far from the accident scene, far from prison life, at home in his soft warm bed beneath a thick, sweet-smelling down comforter and clean cotton sheets. In the dream he opened his eyes and rolled toward the window to see summer sunlight streaming in, turning airborne dust into glittering diamonds, and beside him, his sleeping wife. Helen sensed his gaze and opened her eyes languidly, dreamily, smiling at the sight of him; she reached for him, pulled his face to hers. He caught the fragrance of roses as they kissed. And then he drew back to look at her, admire her, stroke her face, overwhelmed to tearful gratitude to see her eyes serene, vibrant, alive—free of the horrifyingly vacant look of the dying.

He rose, feeling amazingly light on his feet, amazingly strong, and moved to the window to see the sky, blue and cloudless. Below, the small landscaped yard in front of the townhouse bloomed with red roses. The very air seemed saturated with joy. He glanced back at the bed, at the still form of his drowsing wife, smiled, then walked to the bedroom door.

Movement. A blur as a hand shot forward out of nowhere and seized his neck with such momentum that Kimble reeled. He blinked, and as his vision cleared he found himself staring into the broad, hideous face of the one-armed man.

Kimble gasped and opened his eyes to bird song

and streaming sunlight. He sat up stiffly, scattering branches and cardboard, and drew a trembling hand across his brow as he remembered where he was, and what he had to do.

He did not linger. He removed the signs of his stay and hurried into town, determined to find a way to head north once more—home, to Chicago, and the one-armed man.

He committed his fifth crime in a drugstore, where he lifted a pair of scissors and a bottle of Lady Clairol, Precocious Mink, from the shelf. The ease with which he accomplished this disturbed him—he worried he was getting a little too good at petty thievery.

He found a pay phone and used some of his stolen change to make a long-distance phone call.

"Law offices of Gutherie, Morgan and Wainwright."

"Walter Gutherie, please," Kimble said.

"I'm sorry, Mr. Gutherie has left for the day. Would you like his voice mail?"

Kimble hung up.

He took his stolen booty to a nearby gas station rest room and set to work. The results were adequate but hardly flattering. He was frowning at his altered reflection in the broken mirror when he heard the rumble of a large vehicle and voices just outside the scarred, filthy door.

A man shouted. "Get in or we'll never get there. Where's Adam? Adam!"

Behind Kimble, a toilet flushed. He started; he had

thought himself alone, but it was possible that as he was rinsing his head in the scum-filled sink, someone had slipped inside.

A young boy—four or five—stepped out of the stall. He paused to regard Kimble with large, solemn eyes set in a head still too big for the rest of his small body, then rinsed his hands and dashed out.

Kimble followed. The shout had come from the driver of a camper parked at the side of the station. Adam climbed obediently in, but not before Kimble passed from the front of the camper to the back—where he stopped when he saw the Illinois license plate, and the ladder leading to the roof.

In the starkly appointed U.S. Marshal's Office in Chicago, Gerard sat at the conference table with Newman, Renfro, Poole, and Biggs. A stack of twenty-odd files rested on the polished cherry surface to the left of Poole's elbow; to the right, two files remained—the last of the day's work. She picked up the top one on her right, opened it, and passed a photograph to Newman on her left.

"Willis Johnson," she said, as Newman squinted at the photo, then shrugged and passed it across the table to Renfro, who studied it a moment before passing it on to Biggs. "Escaped from Menard February eleven. Here's his mug shot for comparison." The booking photograph followed the same sequence, from Newman to Renfro to Biggs, who held both pictures side by side.

Biggs nodded. "Looks like him."

He proffered both photos to Gerard, who took the most recent but refused the booking shot. There was no need; his eye had recorded Willis Johnson's every feature. He could pick the man out of a crowd of a thousand.

Gerard glanced at the photo no more than a second, then tossed it across the table at Poole. "That ain't the guy," he said, and that was that. Biggs passed the booking shot back to her and Poole refiled both photographs without hesitation or comment. No one questioned the decision, because Gerard had an uncanny ability to see through any disguise to the man beneath.

Gerard moved on to the last topic as Poole set the file atop the stack of twenty and opened the remaining file. "Copeland?"

He held a special place in his heart for Copeland for two reasons: one, because the man was an unnecessarily brutal killer; and two, because he had been on that fateful bus ride to Menard with Richard Kimble.

Renfro leaned forward to share news of progress in the case. "Girlfriend. Left work yesterday, withdrew two hundred dollars from an automatic teller machine—her maximum."

Poole nodded, scanning the contents of Copeland's file. "Car was spotted in East St. Louis."

Gerard leaned back and steepled his hands, thinking. "She run with anybody in the area?"

"None that we can find," Poole said.

"Then keep looking." Gerard straightened in his chair, the signal to leave. The others rose. Gerard picked up the one file he had carried in with him, the one he had been studying of late; as he did, the booking photo of Kimble slipped out, faceup, onto the table. He retrieved it and glanced up to see Newman watching with a curious expression.

He ignored him and called to Poole, who paused in the doorway at the sound of her name. "Poole? You get that transcript of Kimble's trial for me?"

Her dark face revealed no trace of the surprise she must have felt at Gerard's unusual request. He had never before asked for the details of the case—had never been interested, had only wanted to know what was necessary to capture his man. But there was a slight hesitancy in her voice as she answered, "It's on your desk."

Gerard kept his expression impassive. "Thank you." As the others trooped out, he swiveled in his chair toward the wall behind him, and tilted his head to gaze up at the bulletin board full of wanted posters, searching until he found the one set of eyes that intrigued him.

"What's that?"

He jerked his head to see Newman beside him, still wearing a curious expression.

Gerard looked back at Kimble's poster. "Purgatory," he said slowly. "Where the unaccounted souls rest till they either miraculously reappear in the land of the living, or get my approval to be considered dead."

*   *   *

Kimble had thought that the previous night marked the coldest he'd ever been in his life, but as the camper headed north up the highway, the sky clouded over and the wind shifted, bringing arctic air with it. The worst part was his hands, gloveless and exposed to the raw cold as he clung to the roof of the camper, wind flapping inside his stolen clothes.

They rode for hours. Kimble turned his head so he could read the road signs, and watch as they passed over the state line.

By the time they pulled into Sonny's Truck Stop & Diner in central Illinois, Kimble's teeth were chattering and his fingernails were a pronounced shade of blue. He waited for the riders to disembark before he dared crawl down, unseen; his hands were so numb he could scarcely grip the rungs of the ladder.

Just inside the restaurant, he found a pay phone by the rest rooms, and cursed softly when he realized that it was the weekend now and he did not know Walter's unlisted home number. But he had to keep trying. He managed, with some difficulty, to fish a quarter out of his pocket and get it into the slot, and again dialed the one number he could remember, praying that, through some miracle, someone would be in to answer the phone.

This time, a recording answered. "You have reached the law offices of Gutherie, Morgan and Wainwright. Our office hours are nine through five, Monday through Friday. If you would like to leave a message . . ."

Kimble replaced the receiver in its cradle.

He wandered into the dining area and settled at the

counter. The smells of cooking food reminded him of his painful hunger.

The somber little boy from the camper emerged from the men's room, and glanced over at him with owlish surprise. Kimble ducked his head, relieved when the father called out and the boy darted back to the camper.

A waitress with tall, heavily lacquered hair that did not move when she did leaned across the counter and before he could ask, filled his coffee cup, smiling at him with hard, fortyish beauty. "Need to see a menu?"

Kimble forced a faint smile. "Some soup, please."

"Good choice." She winked, marked her pad, and left.

The coffee revived and warmed him. After half a cup, he felt human enough to think more about strategy. The attorney's office would be open Monday, nine A.M. He needed to figure out a way to get to downtown Chicago and get his hands on some more cash to tide him over until then.

A loud clatter came beside him. Kimble glanced in its direction, and up into the face of a surly aproned man busing dishes into a rubber tub. He gazed directly into Kimble's face—a few seconds too long, as though trying to remember where he had seen it before.

Kimble turned away, fighting panic as he lowered his face to his coffee. The dishwasher headed back into the kitchen. Surreptitiously, Kimble glanced around the room to see who else might be able to identify him, and locked stares with an elderly man in worn overalls.

Near the back of the restaurant, a man at the pay phone eyed him as he spoke into the receiver. Kimble froze.

My God, he's calling the police . . .

And then forced himself to draw a deep breath and relax. The man wasn't really staring at him; his eyes weren't focused. He just happened to be looking in Kimble's direction. And the old farmer was just checking out the newcomer in town.

Kimble hoped.

But the paranoia refused to ease its grip. He turned as a steaming bowl of soup was set in front of him on the counter, and glanced up at the waitress—a younger woman, with long hair. The spoon trembled in his unsteady grip as he took a mouthful of chicken noodle and saw, out of the corner of his eye, the older waitress putting on her coat to leave.

Going to the police.

Kimble's heartbeat and breathing quickened, but he stubbornly remained where he was and continued eating. Without food, he wouldn't be able to get much farther. He forced himself to ignore the others around him and glanced up at the small television bolted to the wall behind the counter. The local evening news was on. As he ate, he willed himself to listen to a report on drug busts in Chicago and a lighthearted segment on gourmet pet food, and then suddenly a reporter appeared, standing in front of a startlingly familiar sight: the Barkley Dam.

It was a report on his escape. As the reporter described how U.S. Marshal Samuel Gerard and his team had pursued the fugitive, the booking photograph of Kimble flashed briefly on the screen.

Kimble set down his spoon, fished some dollar bills from his pocket, and slapped them down on the counter. On his way out, he heard the remainder of the report:

According to Deputy Marshal Gerard, Kimble resisted capture by leaping into the deadly waters of the Barkley Dam. He is presumed to have drowned. Local authorities are dragging the reservoir, but so far, no body has been found. . . .

Outside, in the bitter cold, street lamps lit up the parking lot. Kimble walked until he moved out of sight of the diner and into darkness, and then he began to run, sure that someone had spotted him. Sure that it would be only moments before police sirens would be heard in the distance.

He jogged alongside the open highway, heading for the train station he knew lay at the edge of town, wondering how he could manage to slip onto the train bound for Chicago unnoticed.

Less than a mile from the restaurant he had finally begun to relax when he heard the wail of sirens behind him; he ran faster, but the sirens quickly overtook him. He slowed to a jog, realizing there was no outrunning the inevitable. On either side of the highway lay open, unforested fields, offering no place to hide.

By the time the speeding police cruiser neared, he had slowed to a walk, knowing his form was clearly illumined by the steady glare of white headlights.

But the flashing red-and-blue swept past him down the road.

Kimble staggered to a stop, folded his arms around his chest, and bent forward, waiting for his trembling and the pounding of his heart to ease.

He was walking again when a second set of headlights approached, and he was not unnerved by them until the car pulled next to him and the passenger window rolled down.

He hesitated, ready to bolt, until he saw inside the older waitress from the restaurant, the one who had taken his order.

She leaned toward him from behind the steering wheel, and smiled. "Need a ride?"

He studied her for an instant, decided that no guile lay behind her expression. "Which way are you going?"

She lifted an arm and pointed straight ahead—north, Kimble knew. Toward Chicago. Toward home.

It had rained the night before. By dawn, a fine mist hovered above the abandoned field next to the house, and the grass glittered with dew. It was a quiet house in a quiet neighborhood, far removed from town; the only traffic consisted of a garbage truck rumbling slowly down the street, a parked plumbing van, a bag lady picking hurriedly through the garbage before it was hauled away.

In the unmarked G sedan parked across the street, Newman sat beside Renfro. When Gerard unexpectedly yanked open the door, he nearly started out of his skin, but recovered enough to hand Gerard his radio.

Newman was the most recent addition to Gerard's staff, and over the past week, he had grown tired of being constantly reminded of it. He felt himself perfectly competent to handle the work, and wanted to be given a chance to prove himself.

However, this was different: this was life-or-death, and he was beginning to wonder seriously whether he had made a terrible mistake in choosing a career. True, he had trained for action of this sort, and knew the theory, but he had never participated in it. It was one thing to do a training exercise; it was another thing altogether to risk one's life.

He knew he was about to die.

Gerard was stone faced as always as he slid into the front seat; Renfro seemed maddeningly calm as he said, conversationally, "Local officials were about to wet their pants to move in."

"I bet they were," Gerard replied, and raised the radio to his lips. "Where's the woman?"

A squawk of static burst through the mouthpiece and then Biggs's voice replied, "Same room." Newman leaned forward and peered into the plumbing van, where Biggs, dressed in a plumber's coveralls, was leaning his head down to speak into his shoulder mike.

Gerard nodded and said into his radio, "Okay. I'll take front. Biggs and Renfro, rear. Poole—"

The bag lady looked up from the bag of garbage and directed a barely perceptible nod toward the unmarked sedan.

"—handle support," Gerard finished. "I don't want anyone hurt. Stay outside unless called. Radios on three."

Gerard pocketed the radio; he and Renfro checked their weapons. Newman halfheartedly looked over his new service-issue .38 and glanced over at Gerard's new piece: another sexy .40-caliber Glock 22. The number 2 was engraved on the stock. He felt a faint hope at Gerard's omission. "Uh . . . just want me to wait here, sir?"

Gerard scowled as if utterly annoyed by the suggestion, but Newman fancied he saw a glint of amusement in the marshal's eye. "Hell, no. You're with me, Newman. Let's go."

Newman's lips parted slightly in despair. Now he *knew* he was doomed.

The two men silently approached the front of the house. Gerard gave the nod to Newman, and silently mouthed the count: *One, two,* three . . .

Between them, they kicked down the door, splintering the bolt off.

"U.S. marshals!" Gerard bellowed, with such explosive force that Newman involuntarily started. "Down! Down!"

And Newman was running alongside Gerard on sheer adrenaline, knees wobbly, .38 shaking in his hands, but they made it into the living room with textbook-perfect form.

A split-second glimpse of a moving blur down the hall: Copeland.

Newman's heart began thumping in his chest, so hard that he feared he might throw up.

In that same fleeting instant, Copeland was gone, vanished into a back room before Gerard or Newman could fire. A woman in the back began to scream, shrilly, nerve shatteringly. Gerard ignored her and gestured for Newman to head left, toward the door off the living room, while he veered down the main hall into the back bedroom.

Obediently, Newman headed left, praying all the while that Copeland would not see Biggs and Renfro waiting for him out back, that the two men would capture him without firing a shot. He kept moving, moving, eyes scanning every inch of the room, ears alert for any sound, and spoke to his frazzled nerves: it would be all right. They had the jump on Copeland; they were trained professionals. *He* was a trained professional. He was going to be all right . . .

The woman shrieked again, this time hitting a piercing note to shatter glass. At the sound, Newman wheeled into shooting stance. He gathered himself, threw open the door to find a small bedroom, with a second closed door that presumably led out into the hallway, and a third that led either to another closet or to a bathroom. He angled himself, moving forward with the trembling .38 preceding him.

The room was empty; no one in the open closet.

The second door slammed open. Newman pivoted, gun at the ready, and relaxed when he saw Gerard, standing in the hall.

Gerard motioned for Newman to open the third door, then headed back down the hall, to the back bedroom, where the woman still shrieked.

Newman sprung open the door. It led to an empty

bathroom. He drew a breath and relaxed. Copeland was farther back, where Gerard and the others would find him. He, Newman, was safe. With deep relief, he moved toward the hall, then paused as an eerie, skin-crawling sensation crept over him.

He had forgotten the one thing they'd drummed into him during training: Whatever you do, *look behind the open door . . .*

He turned just as Copeland surged out. Before Newman could aim, Copeland struck out, rattler-swift. Newman watched in horror as the .38 arced into the air, and then Copeland had him, twisting his arms to the breaking point behind his back, a huge gleaming knife pressed into the skin at his throat.

Newman closed his eyes and wept tearlessly. Copeland pushed him toward the exit, then paused.

"I got your man!" he screamed in Newman's left ear. "Now I want outta here!"

Copeland stopped, listened for Gerard. Heard nothing, and pulled Newman backward, cold steel biting into his neck. Newman staggered, reduced to abject terror, able to stand only because of Copeland's support.

They backed into the living room. Copeland shouted again. "You hear me? I said, I want out or I'll cut your man's throat!" He wrenched Newman around so that they were angled between the doorway to the bedroom and the entry to the hall. Newman kept his eyes squeezed shut; he could not hear Gerard, could hear nothing but the sound of Copeland's ragged breathing. Copeland tensed, straining to listen.

A loud *clunk* came from the bedroom. Newman opened his eyes as Copeland whipped him around, just in time to see a shoe hit the bedroom floor.

Copeland realized his mistake too late. He had only enough time to whimper as he turned back toward the hall.

Gerard fired point-blank, once, into Copeland's face.

Newman thought his brain and ears had exploded; the noise was sheer, skull-shattering agony. The forty-caliber bullet tore through flesh and cartilage, spattered blood and skull and brain onto Newman.

The knife disappeared; Copeland fell away.

Newman clutched his aching, ringing ears. Dressed in an immodestly gaping bathrobe, the woman ran up behind Gerard. At the sight of her fallen lover, she began to scream again. To Newman, the noise sounded oddly dulled, as if he were listening from inside a fishbowl.

Impassive, utterly unmoved by the act he had just committed, Gerard turned to her and said, with an air of authority as unquestionable as God's, "Shut up."

The woman shut up.

6

By the time the coroner and tactical came to mop up, Newman was back in the car. The adrenaline had worn off, but not the pain. He decided his left eardrum had burst.

Gerard stopped by, holding coffee in a Styrofoam cup. He put his free hand on the car's open window ledge and leaned down to peer at Newman, who still tenderly cupped both ears.

Newman was incensed. Gerard may have been his boss and Newman may have been afraid of him, like everyone else, but at the moment his pain and anger overcame his fear.

"My ear . . ." His voice was high-pitched with indignation. "I can't hear a thing out of it. I can't believe you did that!"

Gerard did not appear to take offense. Calmly, he

asked, "You think I should have bargained with him, don't you?"

"Yes!" Newman replied emphatically. "You could have missed! You could have killed me!"

Gerard broke eye contact and straightened slightly, turning his head just enough to stare out at the open field, where the sun had burned away the mist, but not all of the dew; the grass still sparkled, heavy laden with moisture. He seemed to be thoughtfully considering Newman's words. "Yeah, you're absolutely right. I could have."

Newman fell silent, partially mollified. Gerard turned back to study him with sudden sympathy.

"How bad's your ear?"

"Terrible," Newman said. "I probably have permanent hearing damage."

"Let me see it."

Gerard set the cup of coffee on the car's roof and bent forward; Newman lowered his hands, tilted his head so the offended ear angled slightly upward, and leaned toward him.

Gerard brought his face two inches from Newman's. But instead of peering into the injured ear, he brought his lips level with it and spoke in a loud, distinct tone. "I don't bargain."

Newman clutched the ear and cringed in pain; Gerard withdrew, retrieved his coffee, and walked calmly away while the younger man watched, aghast.

Biggs and Renfro stepped up to where Gerard had stood. They were grinning; they had been watching.

"He likes you," Biggs told Newman.

"Yeah," Renfro said, with the authority of experience. "He *yelled* in my ear."

Newman shuddered, leaned back against the seat, and closed his eyes.

By that morning Kimble had made it to downtown Chicago. Being home was a heady, comforting experience, but he reminded himself that this success did not mean his luck would continue. As he disembarked from the train, transit cops were herding homeless out of the station and onto the streets. Kimble blended in with the crowd, and found himself at La Salle Street Station. He waited in the milling crowd, listening to the rumble of trains, overhead els, and the drone of the P.A. announcing departure times and arrivals. Across the street, a digital bank clock flashed time and temperature. When at last it showed 9:01 A.M., Kimble went to a pay phone kiosk and dialed.

The receptionist answered. Kimble asked for Gutherie and held his breath. He knew it was a risk; Gutherie had not sincerely believed him before, and had no real reason to now. But it was Kimble's best hope, and he was betting on the guilt Gutherie had clearly felt over failing to provide a successful defense. Gutherie had been obviously pained by the thought of Kimble in prison. If he could get through to that guilt and convince Walter to help him, he had it made.

Gutherie came on the line, sounding faintly annoyed at this caller who would not identify himself.

Overwhelmed, Kimble struggled a moment to find his voice. "Walter. It's Richard."

A pause of several seconds. And then Gutherie whispered, "Richard . . ." Louder: "Jesus, why did you run? Running only makes you look guilty."

Kimble felt a faint welling of old, familiar frustration. "I wasn't worrying about appearances, Walter."

"Tell me where you are," Gutherie said quickly. "I'll come meet you so you can turn yourself in."

"I'm not turning myself in," Kimble countered. "I need money."

Gutherie fell silent. When he spoke again, his tone was that of an attorney trying to cover his own ass. "Richard. You're asking me to harbor and aid a convicted felon. I can't help you that way. My advice—both as a friend and as your legal counsel—is for you to give yourself up. Now, tell me—where are you?"

Disappointment mixed with anger settled heavily over Kimble; he sagged against the kiosk, fighting to keep the bitterness from his tone. "St. Louis."

"Give me an address," Gutherie said. "I'll be—"

Kimble hung up.

"**R**ewind it," Gerard said.

Seated at the bank of audio equipment in the media room, Renfro pressed the controls. Biggs and Poole sat beside him; Newman, from time to time reaching out to delicately massage an ear, sat next to Gerard.

"Call came in at nine-oh-one this morning," Biggs said.

Poole glanced from him to Gerard. "We've alerted St. Louis P.D."

Gerard ignored them as the tape rewound. Something about it had set off an alarm in his subconscious; something simply didn't smell right.

Renfro hit play, and Richard Kimble's terse voice filled the air.

Walter. It's Richard.

"Drop their voices," Gerard ordered, just as Gutherie replied, *Richard . . . Jesus . . .*

The background sounds of a busy train station filled the room: the roar of trains, snippets of passerby conversation, the clang of bells, the rumble of traffic passing on the streets beyond.

Gerard leaned forward suddenly. "Listen."

"Trains," Biggs said. "Traffic."

Gerard shook his head. "More. There's a voice in the background." He turned to Renfro. "Play it."

Renfro replayed it, enhancing the background sounds. There came the clang of a bell, grinding, mechanical. And then a voice, this time distinct and unmistakable:

"Next stop, Merchandise Mart . . ."

Eyes wide, Renfro jerked his head toward Gerard. "That's an el announcement!"

"And there's no el in St. Louis," Gerard said. "Ladies and gentlemen, Richard Kimble is in Chicago. Poole, call the St. Louis P.D. and tell them you've made a mistake, then get his artwork out to local police and have C.P.D. check the shelters. Biggs, bring in the detectives that handled his case."

Poole and Biggs stood up.

"I'll prepare the press release," Newman volunteered, rising.

"No," Gerard said. The others stopped to stare at him.

Gerard rose slowly, deliberately, looking from face to face with an intensity calculated to let them know just how serious he was about apprehending Kimble. "They don't know he's alive, and as far as Kimble knows, we don't either. I want to keep it that way as long as we can. Are we clear?"

"Perfectly," Renfro said. The group turned to leave.

"Newman," Gerard said.

Newman turned, eagerness warring with apprehension.

Gerard favored him with a grim smile. "Go to my office and let's officially take Dr. Kimble out of purgatory."

Kimble headed for his next-best hope. Fortunately, Charlie Nichols was enough of a creature of habit to be exactly where Kimble expected him to be at nine-thirty on a weekday morning: at his upscale men's health club in the Loop. Kimble watched from a distance as Nichols exited, nodding at the doorman as he passed. Nichols turned the collar of his camel-hair coat to the cold and stepped into the parking lot, the handle of his squash racquet protruding from his gym bag. He looked the same as always: great. Tan, fit, sixty-dollar haircut. He climbed into his shining Ferrari and pulled out onto the street.

At a stoplight, a homeless man dashed from the curb and began washing Nichols's windshield. Nichols, car phone to his ear, waved him away. He continued, and Nichols switched on his wipers; the man ambled away, cursing.

Kimble stepped off the curb and peered into the driver's-side window. On the other side of the glass, Nichols was scowling. Kimble read his lips:

No, not today, please . . .

And then Nichols's expression went blank with surprise; he gaped in recognition.

Oh my God! Richard . . .

He rolled the window down, his features arranging themselves next into a look of pity. Kimble realized what he must have looked like—the chopped, dyed hair, the stubble, the stained, rumpled clothes. A shivering, homeless bum.

"How're you doing, Charlie?" he asked, with a faint, sheepish grin.

Nichols was still stunned. "You're alive . . ."

"Yeah. And I need help."

"Anything," Nichols answered swiftly.

Kimble gave a sincere, broad smile, the first he could remember meaning since Helen's death, and swallowed hard, remembering Nichols's efforts to help him on the witness stand.

Kimble smiled at his friend. Apologetically, he said, "I need some money. Whatever you've got on you."

"Of course." Nichols pulled out his wallet. "Tell me where you're staying. I'll get you more money. Some clothes. Just give me an address . . ."

"I'll call you," Kimble said.

Nichols dug out the cash and gave the thick wad of twenties to Kimble, who pocketed it without counting. Nichols stared up into his friend's face and said softly, "I know why you came back—to find him. If I can help—"

He reached for Kimble's hand. Kimble took it, startled by its warmth, ashamed that his own was icy.

"Call me," Charlie said softly. "Call me . . ."

"Thanks, Charlie . . ."

Nichols reached in the backseat. "You're freezing, aren't you? Here, take my coat—"

Behind him, a police car popped its siren. Kimble panicked, and ducked into a nearby alleyway; but as he glanced, terrified, behind him, he heard the cop shout at Nichols:

"Hey, buddy—green light. Let's go . . ."

That morning, while Newman and Poole checked the train station and Biggs and Renfro scoured the homeless shelters, Gerard went to Kimble's townhouse alone. It was an opportunity he rarely had—to see undisturbed the most private places Kimble had walked and slept and eaten, to get a feel for the man. Gerard wanted to be alone for the ritual because secretly he believed it helped him establish a mental and emotional link with the escaped prisoner, tapping into that mysterious part of his mind that *knew* but could not reason. He told himself that solitude was necessary for his concentration, but in truth it was also necessary because he feared ridicule.

Most of the furniture was gone; what remained was draped in plastic. Shadows on the wall revealed where paintings had once hung. The thermostat had been set low and the rooms were cold and musty smelling; a fine layer of dust covered everything. In the living room, a handsome grandfather clock stood silent, as if time long ago had ceased. Gerard walked across the echoing hardwood floors, dull and in need of polishing after months of neglect and the footfall of some hundred policemen, investigators, photographers, coroners, marshals. He rifled through boxes and shopping bags filled with Kimble's vast and eclectic book collection and was impressed: everything from medical journals to history, philosophy, and literature. Gerard lifted a volume of short stories and glanced at the cover. The book fell open easily in his hands, as if it had been turned to a particular page many times. Gerard frowned at the story's ominous title: "The Dead."

And then he made himself go up the two flights of stairs to the crime scene. The chalk-powder outline of the victim's body had been vacuumed up, but near the plastic-draped bed, dark red-brown stains marred the wool Chinese carpet.

In the silent gloom, Gerard mentally replayed the scene the way the prosecution had said it happened: Kimble springing on his unsuspecting wife, choking her. She had scratched his face and arm, broken away, and run to the phone, knocking it off the cradle as he fired . . .

And then, assuming she was dead, he had knocked over furniture, carefully arranged what was to be interpreted as signs of a struggle. Casually gone downstairs and sifted through the mail, moved the laundry from the washer to the dryer to make it look as if he had arrived home unsuspecting—had even gotten the wine bottle and glasses and brought them up, to make it look as if he had planned a romantic evening with his wife. And in that brief period of time, she had dialed 911. It had thrown a wrench into Kimble's carefully laid plans; he had meant to have more time to make the crime look like a burglary before calling 911 himself. But he had just enough time to make himself look disheveled, and in his panic, he could invent no better cover story than the one-armed man.

Realizing the police would be there any second, he moved quickly into the second phase of his plan: playing the role of grief-stricken husband. He had lifted his dying victim into his arms and waited until the cops arrived, then launched into his calculatedly touching performance . . .

Gerard released an exasperated sigh. Somehow none of it rang true. He decided, just for the hell of it, to replay the events according to Kimble's account. He moved around the bed and stepped into the closet, still full of a man's and woman's clothes, the shoulders pale with dust. The woman—

He flipped open the file in his hands. Helen Kimble.

Helen was in the closet undressing when Richard

was downstairs. He had come up the stairs, seen a hulking figure hiding behind the door. They had struggled. Kimble had torn off the man's artificial limb, but the man had retrieved it and fled.

Kimble was distracted from following him by his wife's moans. He found her mortally wounded, knew 911 had been called, tried to help her and found he couldn't, held her as she died. Afterward, he had looked up at the police officer with eyes full of stunned grief, the same emotion they had worn in the booking photo . . .

"No," Gerard said, and shook his head, not wanting to spend another second allowing himself to believe that Richard Kimble's alleged hell actually existed, not wanting to experience the depth of that pain. Kimble was guilty, guilty. After all, there was that transcript of the 911 recording. He rifled through the file for it.

Did I hear you right? Your attacker is still in the house? Ma'am?

He's trying to kill me . . .

Will you repeat that, please?

Richard . . . He's trying to kill me . . . my head . . .

Utterly damning. And yet . . . Gerard wished he had the recording itself at that moment. Her voice would have been whispery, barely audible; it would have been extremely difficult to detect any change of inflection in her tone.

Was that the moment at which Kimble had entered the room? Had she been speaking to her husband, *not* the 911 operator, as Kimble had claimed at the trial?

Gerard snapped the file shut and went downstairs.

He sat on the plastic-draped living room couch in front of the cold stone fireplace and stared at empty walls as he tried to imagine what this room had been like when people had lived here—say, four years ago, when there had been a fire roaring in the fireplace and a kid's toys scattered on the floor, and a woman's soft voice . . .

"No," Gerard said, and stood up, suddenly angry at himself. It had been a lousy idea, coming here to Kimble's house alone, a lousy idea to permit himself to entertain the notion of Kimble's innocence for even a second. One couldn't lose one's sense of distance, one's sense of professionalism, or one screwed up, and people died.

I didn't kill my wife.

"That's *not my problem!*" Gerard retorted, and left, slamming the door behind him.

7

It was still morning when Gerard took Poole with him to talk to Kimble's nurse. He was glad he did. Poole had what Gerard thought of as The Look: a menacing intensity in the eyes, combined with a breath of that maniacal deadliness Gerard saw in the faces of killers. The Look could strike fear in the hearts of the most hardened criminals; it was intended to. But Gerard had nurtured and worn The Look so long he could no longer rid himself of it if he wanted to. Poole could, and it always surprised him how soft and reassuring she could seem when she wanted to win the trust of an interviewee.

Angelica Flynn was such a person. She was forty-five, immaculate, with graying auburn hair and an air of competence. She led Gerard and Poole through the plush silver-and-plum-appointed waiting room back to one of the exam rooms and gestured for them to sit on the doctor's stool and the exam bench; they refused. The three of them stood throughout the conversation.

Flynn frosted at once when Gerard flashed his badge; clearly, she was still loyal to Kimble. That, and her air of timid delicacy, made Gerard introduce himself, then shut up and let Poole do the talking. Poole dropped The Look, found Flynn's wavelength, and started asking questions with a quiet, direct competence that precisely matched Flynn's demeanor.

Flynn warmed to her at once. She tilted her freckled face, eyes filling with a distant sorrow as she replied.

"I ran Dr. Kimble's office for twelve years. It took me almost a year to find another job."

Poole nodded sympathetically. "Would you say you knew Dr. Kimble well?"

"Well, of course." Flynn's tone grew indignant. "You can't work for someone every day for twelve years without learning *something* about his character."

"How would you describe his character?"

Flynn's faint smile was tinged with sadness. "Thoughtful. He really cared about his patients, and it showed."

"Did you ever pick up on any tension between him and his wife? Did he ever discuss her?" Poole asked it gingerly, but there was no way to sugarcoat the question, and Flynn frosted again.

"Of *course* he discussed her. All the time. He was

crazy about her. They doted on each other. He was on the phone to her every free minute—"

"Jealous?" Gerard asked.

Flynn turned on him, her upper lip curling slightly. "That's just what the prosecutor did. Tried to twist everything into something ugly, trying to find something that simply wasn't there. He *loved* her. She loved him. They were devoted, and believe me, after the things I've seen husbands and wives try to get away with at the clinics and hospitals in this town—"

"We had to ask," Poole said gently, and the apology in her tone calmed Flynn at once.

Flynn nodded, gazing down at the plum carpeting beneath her feet. She folded her arms and re-met Poole's eyes. "I don't understand. Why are you dragging all this up again? Is Dr. Kimble appealing? Is there going to be a new trial?"

"Dr. Kimble has escaped," Gerard said.

Flynn's eyes widened with hope and fear and surprise. She raised a hand to her lips, held it there a moment, then lowered it to speak. "You'll never catch him."

"Why not?" Poole asked.

"Because he's intelligent."

"We're not as stupid as we look," Gerard countered.

She shot him a look of scorn, then addressed Poole. "Determined, too. Once he gets fixed on something, he sticks with it." She paused, and said passionately, "I'm glad he's free. He doesn't deserve to be in prison. He's a good man."

A hint of The Look shimmered over Poole's face. "Ms. Flynn, the man is a convicted murderer."

She drew herself up to her full height. "I can't accept that."

"Would you help him if he came to you for help?" Gerard asked.

She hesitated, averting her eyes lest the answer in them betray her. Finally, she said, "He wouldn't do that."

Gerard could not keep the edge of irony from his tone. "You sound very sure of that."

She looked him in the eye with a gaze as hard, as immovable as his own. Gerard was impressed. "He wouldn't put me or anybody else in that position," Flynn said. "He'd either do it on his own or fail. That's just his way."

In the surgeons' locker room just off the Chicago Memorial O.R., Dr. Jacob Roberts wriggled out of his pastel-blue scrub shirt and sat heavily on the bench, his well-padded chest and stomach settling into three thick, pasty folds.

Gerard and Biggs hovered a polite distance away. Roberts had not been all that close to Kimble—he had not been a friend. But he had worked alongside Kimble enough years to shed some light on the case. And Gerard wanted to hear from someone who would not rush to Kimble's defense. According to Angelica Flynn, Kimble had once beaten Roberts out for some award, and Roberts still nursed a grudge.

Roberts wadded up his shirt and threw it at the

hamper. "Just how much do you know about Richard Kimble?" His tone was thick with exhaustion; Gerard assumed he'd been in surgery all night.

"That's our question to you, sir," Gerard replied. "If you know of anything you think would be helpful to our investigation—"

"Kimble was in the navy when he was young," Roberts said, rubbing his face. The statement terminated in a yawn. "Did you know that?"

"Two years," Biggs said, "then he left to go to college, then medical school."

Roberts's lips curved into a weary, knowing smirk. "I saw that bit about him jumping in the dam. I could have told you he wasn't dead. Besides, the guy was a helluva swimmer."

"University swim team," Biggs said.

"I laughed my ass off when I heard that dam story. That's Richard . . ."

Gerard leaned forward, suddenly intense, and held Roberts's gaze. "Do you think he's guilty?"

Roberts shrugged, looked away. "I don't know." He sighed. "I *do* know R. K.'s one smart, cold son of a bitch. If he made up his mind that he wanted to do her . . . then he did her, no question."

Gerard straightened. "Thank you, Dr. Roberts. If you hear from Dr. Kimble—"

Roberts guffawed. "Oh, I won't be hearing from him. Don't worry. He's too damned stubborn to come to *me* for help . . ."

"Who would he go to?"

"Nobody, if he could get away with it." Roberts paused, settling his bulk against the wall as he stared off into the distance, thinking. "If he *had* to, though . . ." He glanced at Gerard. "I'd talk to Charlie Nichols, if I were you."

Despite his rumpled appearance, Kimble blended easily into the corridor traffic at Cook County Hospital, moving with the authority of someone long accustomed to striding down hospital halls. He took careful note of their security measures, then lingered just long enough at the directory by the main elevator bank to ensure that the place he sought was still located where he remembered it to be, years ago, when he had worked here as an intern.

At an elbow in the corridor, he stopped at the wall sign that read

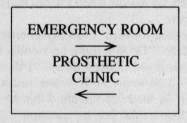

and paused as a mental image flashed: himself, staring in horror at the hollow limb in his hands, its interior a mechanical lace of wire and electrodes—then looking up into the startled, contorted face of Helen's killer . . .

He followed the sign, found the waiting room and sat, peering over the cover of a *People* magazine at

his destination on the other side of the glass walls—
a computer room and records area. Nearby, a patient
sitting with a detached prosthetic arm on his lap
smiled over at Kimble.

"Good morning."

"Good morning," Kimble replied, and pretended
to return to reading his magazine, but he could see
from the corner of his eye the man studying him, as
though trying to solve the puzzle of why an able-
bodied person had come to such a place.

Kimble put down the magazine and left.

He did not leave the hospital, but proceeded directly to the next step. He'd had plenty of time since
his escape to work out his plan in great detail. Not
everything had gone as well as he'd hoped—Gutherie had been a major disappointment—but Nichols
had provided the money that made the rest of the
plan possible.

Kimble found his way to the janitors' room, brush-
ing shoulders with exiting hospital staff. He moved
past lockers, shelves, and boxes stacked with cleaning supplies, and stopped at the bulletin board which
listed the work schedules, vacation leaves, and locker
numbers. A pencil was attached to the board by a
dirty string; Kimble glanced furtively over his shoulder and made a few strategic erasures and additions.
All he needed was a couple of days . . .

Behind him, a locker slammed. Kimble pivoted to
see one of the workers moving off to the showers.
His locker remained slightly ajar from the impact;
part of a collar with a clip-on plastic I.D. protruded.

He could not pass up the opportunity. Glancing

over his shoulder to be sure the room was empty, he slipped the shirt and I.D. from the locker.

Crime number six.

The plan was in place. Kimble left the hospital and made his way to a nearby Salvation Army second-hand store and bought appropriate janitorial attire: green pants to match the shirt, work shoes. On his way out of the store, he noticed a handwritten rent ad on the wall and stuck it into his pocket.

The next stop was a take-your-own photo booth in front of a Wal-Mart. Then it was on to the address in the ad, a four-story tenement on a garbage-lined street.

A teenager with a punk haircut and an earring in his nose answered; at the sight of Kimble, he turned and shouted for his grandmother, an aged Polish woman, stockings rolled down to her shins.

The basement room was cold and grim but cheap, and the ancient landlady pocketed his cash with no questions asked. He sat on the bed and used stolen scissors to cut out his photograph, and carefully inserted it into the stolen hospital I.D.

And then he allowed himself a short nap to ease the exhaustion of endless walking combined with a sleepless night. He dreamed again of that electrifying moment when the killer's arm came off in his hand. Kimble tossed the arm aside and reached again for the elusive killer; the man twisted, and this time another arm came free, as hollow as the first . . . and then a leg, and then the man's head, until Kimble stood in a pile of empty body parts.

And the man's detached head began laughing . . .

Kimble woke with a shudder, and rose, despite the fact that the sun was still high in the sky.

Gerard headed with Biggs to Chicago Memorial Hospital, where they waited for the administrative head of pathology, Dr. Charles Nichols, outside his office. According to Kimble's file, Angelica Flynn, and Jacob Roberts, Nichols was supposed to have been one of Kimble's closest friends. Certainly, as he strode past his secretary's desk toward his office, only to be stopped and confronted by the two waiting men, he eyed them with the same resentment Gerard had sensed emanating from Flynn.

He led them into his *Architectural Digest* office.

"Sit down," Nichols said, motioning to chairs after Biggs and Gerard had introduced themselves. He made no move to shake the officers' hands, but closed the door behind them, then slipped off his white lab coat and switched it for the dark suit coat hanging from the hook behind the door. He seemed annoyed but not at all nervous.

The two marshals did not sit. Nichols did not repeat his offer, but walked over to stand behind his blindingly polished, overlarge desk and study his two visitors with narrowed eyes.

Biggs opened his mouth to speak, but Nichols interrupted tersely.

"I suppose this has to do with Richard Kimble."

"What makes you think that?" Gerard asked.

"Because I saw him two days ago."

Biggs jerked up, startled, looking as if Nichols had

just bitten him. Gerard leaned forward slowly, almost imperceptibly, sizing up Nichols the way a lion would prey.

"He stopped me in my car. I gave him some money—what I had on me," Nichols said calmly, "and spoke with him for only a couple of minutes."

"Where was this?" Gerard fired.

"Outside our tennis"—Nichols paused to correct himself—"*my* tennis club. Near the Loop. I don't recall the exact address, but my secretary can write it down for you."

"Did he ask you for help?" Restless, Gerard began to wander around the room, absorbing the details. There were few. The office was too sterile, too interior decorator-ish. Like Nichols, too pretty. Gerard angled his head just enough to see the silver-framed photograph on Nichols's desk, of a blond woman—lean and model-gorgeous, like Nichols. Like the office.

"I volunteered," Nichols said, with quiet self-righteousness. "He wouldn't accept it."

Gerard and Biggs glanced at each other; this much rang true, as it echoed Nurse Flynn's statement. "Why do you think he came back to Chicago?"

"He didn't tell me."

Biggs and Gerard shared a look of ill-concealed annoyance. "I didn't ask you that, sir." Gerard turned from a framed, yellowed photo on the wall, of a much younger Richard Kimble and Charles Nichols. The label beneath read, "Cook County Medical interns, 1975." "I'm sure he was trying to protect you from having to lie for him. If you're really his friend, you'll help us bring him in unharmed."

He wandered over to a bookcase and scanned the group of framed photographs, pausing at a more recent one of Nichols standing proudly beside a gleaming Ferrari.

Nichols's tone was scornful. "Why? So he can go to prison and wait for his number to be called? If you want help, gentlemen, you've come to the wrong man."

Gerard swiveled his head to face Nichols and fastened The Look on him, speaking quickly in a tone deceptively soft and polite. "Doctor . . . Last year, the U.S. Marshal's Office closed out eleven thousand three hundred warrants. Ten thousand nine hundred seventy-five of those were captured. Twenty-eight others, however, *thought* they were smarter than us. Now they're dead." He paused to let Nichols think about it, then nodded at the photograph and added: "Nice car."

And he left with Biggs, knowing that his words would make absolutely no difference. Kimble would contact Nichols again, and Nichols would help him.

Which, whether Nichols knew it or not, would lead the U.S. marshals straight to Kimble.

In the corridor, Gerard turned to Biggs. "Stay on him."

Kimble went on duty at the hospital at the precise time he had penciled on the janitorial schedule: evening shift. It came sooner, and besides, he somehow felt safer working under the cover of night, when there was less staff around. He found a mop, dolly, and bucket, and set to swabbing the deck at a corridor that terminated ten feet away in a door marked "Prosthetic Clinic. Restricted Area."

He inched toward the doorway as he mopped, keeping a wary eye out for traffic. So far, so good. The halls were dead silent . . .

. . . until he heard footsteps behind him and turned to see a young white-coated doctor slip, regain her balance, and look up at him with a puzzled frown.

"Where's Rudy?"

Kimble ducked his head. "They said he's sick."

She glanced around, still frowning, auburn hair swinging. "Didn't they tell you to put up the sign?"

"Uhhh . . ." Kimble shook his head, still trying to keep his face averted. "No. They didn't."

She shot him a dirty look and made a clicking sound of disgust as she moved off. "Put up the 'wet floor' sign before someone gets hurt." And she opened her file folder and became immediately absorbed in whatever she was reading.

"Asshole," Kimble muttered. And immediately regretted it. She hadn't been that rude, but his nerves were on edge, and the name-calling helped release some of the pent-up tension.

She stopped in mid-stride, stiffened, and looked over her shoulder at him with pursed lips. "*What* did you say?"

"Nothing." Kimble hunched over and started vigorously mopping.

Her eyes narrowed; she lingered an instant, then turned and strode off toward the E.R.

He waited until she was out of sight, and then he silently set the mop handle down and headed for the dimly lit prosthetics lab. Prosthetic arms, hands, and legs hung from the ceiling; the counters were covered with cables and electronic equipment. Kimble moved from the lab into an office area, past a computer room, to the file storage area. He had just put his hand on the door leading to the records area when a woman's voice behind him said, "Hey, Ricky . . . Weren't you just in here?"

Kimble turned, trying not to appear nervous. Behind him stood one of the technicians, a large bespectacled woman who held a partially constructed prosthetic arm in one hand. She blinked owlishly at him.

"Sorry. I thought you were Ricky."

"No . . . I've got to clean the blinds in the office. Want me to wait till you're finished?"

"Naw . . ." She gestured with the artificial arm. "Got a patient coming in for a fitting in a couple days and I've got to finish it. I'm gonna be here all night. You won't bother me."

She went back to her workstation and slipped on a headset, nodding to the beat and humming tunelessly while she carefully painted a section of the arm.

Keeping one eye on the technician, Kimble pretended to clean the blinds. He worked his way deliberately toward the records area, and after checking to be sure she was still engrossed in her work, slipped inside.

He silently slid open file drawers until he found the one containing what he needed: case photographs marked by date. He did not take patient files; there were hundreds of those, and it would take weeks to sort through them looking for one man. Kimble was looking for something else—something he would recognize only when he found it.

On the shelf atop the steel filing cabinets, he saw the *Prosthetic Clinic Operations Manual.* He slipped it and files into a plastic trash can, then glanced up to see that the technician had left her workstation.

Kimble had the eerie sensation he was being watched. Pulse quickening, he bent over the trash can and pretended to search through it for something.

"Lose something?"

He wheeled to see the technician standing behind him, bowl in her hand. "Yeah. I dropped my rag." He fumbled through the papers a bit more, then pretended to discover the rag, which lay beside the can, where he had dropped it. "Here it is." He straightened, showing it to the tech, praying his hand would not begin to shake.

She seemed cheerfully oblivious of his anxiety. "You like chili? I've got a crock over there. I make it really hot."

Kimble released a long, silent sigh as his body released its tension. "Thanks, but no . . ."

She shrugged. "Well, help yourself if you get hungry."

In the corridor, Kimble pulled the files and manual from the plastic trash can and slipped them beneath the waistband of his pants, then pulled his jacket over them. He carried the mop and bucket to the janitor's closet in the corridor, then hurried to the elevator banks and waited, rearranging the files slightly when they shifted beneath his clothes.

Just as the elevator doors opened, he sensed someone at his elbow. He turned to see the young doctor who had slipped earlier on the wet floor, and as they stepped together onto the elevator, he caught the name on her I.D.: Anne Eastman.

Kimble moved to the opposite side of the elevator, hoping that Eastman would be too preoccupied to notice him. Bad enough that she had spoken with him once; a second conversation guaranteed that she would be sure to remember him, well enough for a positive I.D.

They rode in silence a few seconds; and then Kimble's hopes were dashed when Eastman said softly, "Hey, how're you doing?" Her tone was warm, friendly, a far cry from her earlier brusqueness. Kimble understood. He had seen her heading toward the E.R., where she probably worked—not an easy rotation. The pressure of frantically trying to save lives—and sometimes failing—frayed nerves. She probably realized she had snapped and was trying to be nice to him now, by way of apology.

He could not afford her kindness, her friendship, despite the fact that her conversational opening made him realize his desperate loneliness. It would not have been safe for either of them, and so he did not meet her eyes, but stared straight ahead at the floor indicator, and said shortly, "Fine."

"You find that sign?" Her tone grew teasing; she was not accusing, only reminding.

He could not resist smiling faintly, and gave her a sidewise glance. "Yes, I did."

Her lips twitched as they curved upward. "You called me an asshole."

He flushed, looked away, and mumbled sheepishly, "Excuse me. I was having a bad shift."

"That makes two of us," Eastman said, and gave a little laugh. Kimble smiled, wistful that he could not afford to get to know this person; there was an air of intensity, of dedication, that reminded him of Kathy Wahlund—and, he realized with a small mental start, himself.

The elevator stopped and opened onto the ground level. Kimble stepped off, and Eastman walked with him.

"You worked at other hospitals?" she asked.

He felt torn; he wanted to talk to her, wanted to allow himself the pleasure of conversation with her, but he knew he would have to avoid ever talking to her again, ever seeing her. He would have to extricate himself as quickly as possible. "Lots of them, over the years," he replied. "Here, long ago. Hasn't changed much."

The corridor branched. He moved toward it, away from her, signaling that their talk was at an end. Eastman seemed vaguely disappointed. She turned and watched him leave. "I bet it hasn't. See you."

On his way out the main entrance, someone shoved a flier into his hand and murmured something about health seminars at the hospital. He thought

126

nothing of it, folded the flier and tucked it into his jacket pocket, and walked out into the darkness, alone.

Kimble took the el back to his basement apartment and spent the next several hours sorting through photographs of prosthetics, making notes on cable attachments, joints, electronics, pins, straps, searching for anything that would lead him to Helen's killer. He knew he could not go through every single patient file since the Prosthetic Clinic had opened— there were far too many. What he needed was to familiarize himself with the terminology and how the clinic organized their data, then decide in his own mind the best way to narrow his search. Once he got to the computer, there would not be much time. He would need to know precisely what he was looking for.

But there was more to it than that. Intuition told him that there was a key—something stored deep in his memory, half forgotten—that would help him locate the killer; a key that could be found somewhere in the hundreds of photographs.

He struggled the entire morning through the files. By late afternoon, he had not slept, and suffered from exhaustion and eyestrain.

He rose, stepping carefully so as not to displace the photographs spread over the bed and floor, and made his way to the sink, where he wet a washrag with icy tap water, then returned to the bed and lay amid the files with the cloth covering his face.

The thought that he was missing something, something lurking just beneath the surface of his memory, still troubled him. Yet trying to force it did not work. He blanked the worry from his mind, let it go, let himself drift.

In the cold damp darkness, the present receded, and he was back in the townhouse, pumped full of adrenaline, his grip closing on something too cool, too unyielding to be human flesh . . .

(Heart hammering as he reached out toward the hulk fleeing toward the shadows. Caught the arm. Jerked. Twisted, with a powerful fury that might have fractured human bone. Sudden absence of resistance in his grasp, the arm coming loose in the man's sleeve. In the dimness, the man's face contorting with pain.

Himself, gazing down stunned at the arm in his hands . . .)

Beneath the damp washcloth, Kimble's breathing quickened. He had not earlier remembered the man reacting in pain before; he had been too stunned to notice. Perhaps there were other things he might remember to help him with the search, if only he could make himself recall . . .

Again.

(The touch of cool, false flesh. Kimble pulling. Harder. Twisting. Wrenching. Sense of something snapping, loosening, the arm free in his hands. The man reacting with pain. Staring, startled, back at Kimble and then running for the stairs.

Helen's voice had come then, stopping Kimble, but he forced himself now to ignore the sound of her voice, to hear the one-armed man's fleeing footsteps descending the stairs, on the landing, door opening, and then the slam . . .)

Kimble sat up, pulled the wet rag from his face.

Outside the tenement building, a car door had slammed; on the sidewalk, footsteps sounded, rapid and picking up speed, moving toward the apartment.

He hurried to the basement window.

He saw the tires, first at eye level, and then he looked up and saw that they were attached to police cruisers, parked with doors open and motors still running in front of the tenement.

Kimble sagged as if kicked in the chest and released a lungful of air as he recoiled from the window. Instinctively, he wheeled and dashed toward the back door. He almost yanked it open, but paused just long enough to see, through the dirty glass, the cops waiting in the rear courtyard.

He staggered gasping toward the front, only to find himself staring again at the cops massing on the front sidewalk for the assault. He circled helplessly inside the room, his breath coming in sharp little moans. There was no grating, no tunnels leading out to freedom this time. All exits led to the police.

There was nothing to do except wait. In his panicked daze, Kimble wondered whether they would shoot him. He was unarmed, but the police had no way of knowing that; if he held perfectly still, perhaps they would not fire.

And then he considered that perhaps he *should* move. If they took him to prison, he would never be able to find the one-armed man. And he had come too close now . . .

Unsure what to do, Kimble watched in a cold sweat as the police charged the house.

But instead of sweeping down the basement stairs and kicking in his door, the cops thundered up the front steps, into the house overhead.

He laughed, a horrid, tortured sound that held no joy. The cops had screwed up and gone upstairs. Maybe he could slip past . . .

Overhead he heard them shouting.

Pounding on the upstairs door. Noise as the door opened.

Kimble's eye caught movement outside the back door. As he watched, the landlady's grandson dashed out into the back courtyard—then froze at the sight of the cops, wheeled, and headed for Kimble's basement door.

He recoiled as the teenager reached for the door—only to be grabbed by a cop and yanked away.

Kimble moved back, unseen, and listened to the sounds of the scuffle, and the younger man's high-pitched, tearful wailing. He followed the sounds around to the front of the building and watched the cops shove the young man into a waiting squad car as the landlady followed, weeping.

He leaned trembling against the cold damp wall and closed his eyes.

8

"Tell me about the one-armed man," Gerard said.

He sat in his office across from Detectives Kelly and Rosetti, the men who had questioned Richard Kimble the night of his wife's murder. Renfro and Biggs hovered nearby, listening. The questioning had gone very amicably, so far. Gerard had let his deputies do most of the talking so that Rosetti and Kelly felt at ease.

Renfro: *Was there anything in your initial investigation that would make you think Kimble would come back to Chicago?*

Rosetti: *The man definitely has friends here.*

Gerard had listened, and watched. The part in Kelly's slicked hair was uneven. On his ruddy cheek, a patch of graying stubble, missed during his morning shave, glistened when it caught the light, and his collar, the top button undone, gaped open above his loosened tie. Gerard wondered whether the same careless attitude carried over into the man's work. Rosetti was neater, but passive, bland; too easily influenced by Kelly.

Biggs: *What about lady friends?*

Kelly: *Not that we found.*

And then Gerard could resist no longer and dropped the bombshell about the one-armed man. Kelly and Rosetti shared a look; Rosetti snickered.

"Right. You ever been downwind of a stockyard when the breeze is blowing?" Kelly asked, with a cheerful smugness Gerard did not like. "That's where we were sitting when Richard Kimble told that one."

"There's no record of any investigation of the matter in your files," Gerard countered coolly. It was the real reason he had called them both in.

Kelly's easygoing expression hardened faintly. "That's because it had no basis in fact. His people supposedly contacted over one hundred amputees. They couldn't find him."

Gerard leaned forward a half inch and fastened The Look on Kelly. "You're telling me it never occurred to you to check out the story?"

The detective squirmed slightly in his chair; his tone grew defensive. "No, because not one trace of forensic evidence supported the one-armed-man theory. Everything pointed to Kimble."

"Thank you both," Gerard said, with a soft civility that did not attempt to veil his scorn. "We'll call you if we need any more information."

* * *

Kimble knew that going through patient files one at a time would be a hopeless task—he needed to get to the Prosthetic Clinic's computer records. But he had hoped first to glean some more insight from the photos of prosthetics to help him narrow his search; his intuition stubbornly insisted that the key lay there. But the sun was setting, and time was running out. He rose and dressed in his janitor's clothes for work.

He found himself having to repress the hope that he might have another chance to talk to Anne Eastman. It was too risky; he told himself that he would have to avoid her.

He reported to the hospital just as the graveyard shift began, got his trash cart from the janitor's closet, and headed down the corridor for the Prosthetic Clinic. Just outside, two uniformed police officers stood talking; Kimble did a one-eighty and headed in the opposite direction, toward the emergency room.

The hallway outside the E.R. was jammed with traffic. Doctors, orderlies, nurses were all running toward the emergency room; Kimble peered through the open double doorway to the waiting room and saw a dozen gurneys being wheeled in by paramedics.

The P.A. blared overhead. "Dr. Clepper-Faith, please report to emergency STAT. Dr. Clepper-Faith . . . Dr. Choojitarom, please report to emergency STAT . . . Dr. Moroz, please report . . ."

Once the cops left, it would be the perfect opportunity to head for the Prosthetic Clinic unobserved, while everyone was distracted—but despite himself, Kimble's attention was pulled to the drama unfolding at the other end of the corridor. He pushed the cart against the wall, out of the way of moving bodies, and walked to the E.R. entrance.

Anne Eastman had just arrived. She did not notice Kimble, but walked swiftly beside an orderly who wheeled a gurney. On the gurney lay a young boy—conscious, glassy eyed with pain and fear. Eastman smiled down at the boy, touched his hand reassuringly, then spoke rapid-fire to the orderly.

"What happened?"

"A bus flipped off the overpass," the orderly said breathlessly. "Got at least twenty more coming in."

"What about this one here?" She nodded at the boy.

"Fractured sternum. X ray's coming up."

Eastman picked up the chart hanging on the foot of the gurney and studied it. She replaced it, and called, in a clear, commanding voice, "Okay, we've got to get some room in this hallway, people."

Orderlies began moving the less critical patients out of the hall. The E.R. doors flew open again; more stretchers rolled in, more white-coated figures went into motion. The corridor filled with moans and wails as the scene verged on utter chaos. Eastman directed traffic as she moved rapidly between the bleeding victims. She turned and spotted Kimble, who tried unsuccessfully to duck out of sight.

"Hey! Take this one up the hall to Critical Care."

Kimble nodded and began wheeling the gurney up

the hall; the boy lying on it—maybe five, six years old—groaned softly as he reached for his sternum, then recoiled in pain. A nurse laid a fresh set of X rays directly on the boy's chest as she ran past without even slowing. Kimble craned his neck to get a good look at them; what he saw there alarmed him.

The boy groaned again, and Kimble glanced down at him and smiled, slipping effortlessly into his old bedside manner. "How're you doing, champ? What hurts?"

The boy looked up at him with wide, bright eyes. "My chest. My chest hurts."

Kimble scanned the hall quickly, then reached down and, with an experienced surgeon's deft precision and economy of movement, probed the sternum and rib cage. "There?"

The boy nodded, grimacing. Kimble studied the X ray again, not liking what he saw; the sternum had fractured so that part of it pressed down, putting pressure in the area of the aorta.

He rolled the boy down the hall into an empty elevator and ran his finger over the floor buttons, bypassing the one for the third floor, where the CCU was located. Instead, he pressed the button marked "4"—fourth floor, Surgery.

When the doors closed over them, Kimble lifted the chart from the foot of the gurney and scribbled an order.

D own the hall, Anne Eastman watched in utter amazement as the new janitor studied the patient's X ray.

He had intrigued her from the moment she had glanced up from her undignified slip on the just-mopped floor and seen him watching her with concern. He had an air of mystery about him, an awkwardness and a strange grace, as if he were very much out of place in these hospital corridors and at the same time very much at home in them. Eastman sensed an air of tragedy, too. From his speech, he seemed far too educated for an entry-level janitorial position; she decided that the unspoken sorrow had something to do with it.

The thought of him both troubled and attracted her. In the few moments' pause she sometimes got between emergencies, she found herself that night thinking of him.

Then the accident victims had started arriving, and there had been no time to think. Eastman watched as the janitor frowned at the X ray, then reached down to gently probe the boy's injury, with the skill and practiced ease of a trained physician.

She craned her neck, tried to negotiate through incoming patients and gurneys to get a better look, but the janitor was gone. An orderly called out to her for help, and Eastman turned back to her work, the new janitor once again forgotten.

"**H**ang in there," Kimble said cheerfully, as he rolled the gurney carrying the boy at top emergency stride—more than a walk, not quite a run—off the elevator. "We're just going for a little ride." The boy's face was taut with pain, but he was still alert enough to take in the ride, his big eyes noting the swift passage of doorways and overhead lights with a muted delight that said if he hadn't been hurting so bad, he would be enjoying this.

Kimble knew that, on one level, what he was doing was stupid. He was risking everything; if anyone ever figured out who had written the order—

But they would not. He knew how hospitals worked; he knew that the crisis downstairs would keep them too busy to question the unfamiliar handwriting. All that mattered now was saving lives.

It was worth it, if only he could save a parent from hearing the same terrible words he had heard, almost four years before: *We're so sorry. It happened so quickly. By the time we got to him, it was too late* . . . If he could save a mother from having to go through what Helen had, in that awful moment in the emergency room corridor, when she had read of her son's death in Kimble's grief-filled eyes . . .

This kid would make it, even if it meant Kimble had to broadcast his true identity over the hospital P.A.

When they finally arrived at the O.R. entrance, Kimble had to remind himself that he was no longer authorized to enter.

A scrub-suited surgeon, mask half-untied and hanging from his chin, came striding out of the O.R. Kimble stopped him at once and gestured him over to the gurney. "They just sent this one up."

The surgeon gave Kimble's janitor's outfit a critical once-over and lifted an eyebrow. "Looks like they've got everyone working tonight." He lifted the boy's chart and the X ray from the gurney, and his expression immediately darkened. Kimble felt a surge of relief. This man was experienced, competent; he understood the seriousness of the situation. The boy was in good hands.

"Bob!" the surgeon called to the O.R. nurse. "Take this one into room four, stat!"

By the time he looked up, Kimble was gone.

Kimble hurried back to the first-floor wing, found his janitor's cart, and wheeled it into the Prosthetic Clinic. The friendly technician from the night before was there, Walkman headphones in place; she waved as Kimble passed in front of her with the cart. He waved back, pushed the cart into the glass-walled computer room, and shut the door. Blinds covered the glass walls; Kimble closed them, as if he intended to dust them, then went immediately over to the computer and switched it on.

He was no programmer, but he had enough rudimentary computer skills to look in the directories for program files. Most of the file names were enigmatic; the first one Kimble loaded up was not what he was looking for. He exited the program and went back to scanning directories.

And then he saw the file he was looking for—a program called demosrch.exe. At the prompt, Kimble typed "demosrch"; the screen blanked for a second, and then flashed the following words:

CLIENT DEMOGRAPHIC ORGANIZER SEARCH BY: AGE, SEX, RACE, LIMB, OR OTHER?

"Yes!" Kimble hissed exultantly, and typed in:

SEX: MALE
AGE: 35–40
RACE: CAUCASIAN
LIMB: RIGHT ARM
OTHER: POINT OF REPLACEMENT: MID-
   HUMERUS
GRIP SPAN:

He paused, and closed his eyes, remembering the words of the forensic technician during the trial:

. . . the span of the choke mark on the deceased's neck was two hundred thirty millimeters across— precisely the span of Dr. Kimble's own grip . . .

Kimble opened his eyes and keyed in "225–235." A "PLEASE WAIT" message flashed on the screen; the hard drive light flashed as the computer hummed, processing. He hunched over the monitor as the screen changed again.

NUMBER OF POSSIBLE CANDIDATES: 75.
DO YOU WISH TO SUBDIVIDE?

"Seventy-five?" he whispered. Obviously, the program accessed a nationwide databank. "Hell, yes."

He thought for a moment, then added another defining characteristic—"Residence: Illinois."

The green hard drive light flashed again. Kimble straightened and rattled the blinds, to make it seem as though he was cleaning them. He leaned down again as the words on the monitor screen scrolled.

NUMBER OF POSSIBLE CANDIDATES: 21.

Kimble frowned at the number; twenty-one was too many. He simply didn't have the time to investigate that many individuals. Gerard was probably already too close. He rubbed a hand wearily across his eyes and tried to concentrate.

There had to be a faster way.

He closed his eyes, returned to the memory of the artificial arm coming free in his hand at mid-humerus. The man staring back at him, startled, tearing the prosthesis from Kimble's grip and running away with it . . .

Intuition told him the key was there. *Had* to be there. He sensed he was aggravatingly close to figuring it out, but still the answer eluded him. However, he suspected he knew where he would find it.

Kimble lifted a slat with a finger and peered out into the empty corridor.

The crisis in the E.R. had wound down. Patients had been tended to, processed, and released or whisked off to surgery, the Critical Care Unit, or a hospital room. Feeling drained now that the adrenaline surge had worn off, Anne Eastman moved slowly through the corridors, checking on patients.

She made her way through the CCU, murmuring encouragement to the patients who could hear her, and even those who couldn't. On her way out, she paused in the doorway; something was not right. She frowned, searching her weary memory, and then realized—the boy with the fractured sternum had disappeared. She felt the sudden sinking feeling of loss she always did when a patient died; he was just a little kid, so young. She hated to think—

The unit nurse, Gladys O'Malley, passed by. Eastman reached out and touched her on the shoulder, speaking in the hushed tone inspired by the silence of the CCU. "Gladys. Where's the boy I sent down with the janitor?"

She expected Gladys's blue eyes to cloud at that, and steeled herself to hear bad news. Instead, Gladys looked at her blankly. "What boy?"

"The one with the fractured sternum."

The nurse's gaze swept over the silent, supine patients surrounding them; she turned back toward the doctor, at a loss, and shook her head. "He never came in here."

A sudden chill descended over Eastman. The janitor had seemed like such a decent, intelligent person that she had trusted him—but her mind filled with horrible thoughts. Was he some sort of psychotic who had abducted the boy?

No; impossible. He simply did not seem capable of such a thing. Perhaps in the excitement he had misunderstood her, or perhaps she had been so distracted she had ordered him to do the wrong thing— but that seemed unlikely. Still, if he wasn't in the CCU, then where the hell could he possibly be?

She went on a hunch and dashed up the stairs to surgery; by the time she made it to the fourth floor, she was breathing hard. Dave Jensen, one of the resident surgeons, stood at the O.R. entrance frowning down at a chart in his hand.

"Dave," Eastman gasped. "Did you see a janitor come by earlier?"

Dave glanced up, still distracted, barely registering her presence. "Yeah, he brought a kid down." He handed her the chart. "You write that one up, Anne? I couldn't make out the signature . . ."

Eastman stared down at the medical terminology. There was no doubt in her mind that the order had been written by an M.D. "No," she said, thrusting it back at Jensen, who didn't take it. "I saw—"

Jensen cut her off, turning hastily toward the O.R. "Whoever did knew what the hell he was doing. Kid's a hair away from a ruptured aorta."

He strode back into the operating room. Eastman remained, gaping after him, then down at the orders in her hand.

Kimble stole into the prosthetic storage room, gazing up at the artificial limbs hanging from the ceiling. He found an arm that extended beyond the mid-humerus and took it down.

He began to work the elbow joint,

(the feel of the cool nonliving skin beneath his fingers, the feel of resistance as he pulled, then twisted . . .)

noticing how it moved. And then he wrenched it, hard. Harder, so that it strained at an awkward angle—the same awkward angle he had seen the night of January 20.

(Harder. He had wrenched it harder that night, and in the shadows seen the man grimace in pain, until at last, as he pulled, with a strength born of terror, fury, and desperation, the arm had come free . . .)

Kimble pressed his lips together tightly and twisted with all his strength, forcing the arm into the unnatural position he remembered. The internal hinges in the elbow buckled, then snapped; the forearm sagged, suddenly limp.

Kimble's thinned lips curved in an unhappily triumphant smile. The man's prosthetic joint had broken that night.

He hung the arm back on the ceiling and hurried silently back to the computer room. This time he requested the joint repair list between January 21 and February 1.

Pay dirt. Five names. Kimble hit print, reached over to switch on the printer, then peered through the blinds across the hall at the headphoned technician, who did not react.

In less than a minute, the five names printed out. Kimble tore the paper from the printer and slipped it into his pocket, then hurried out into the corridor. He did not bother to retrieve his cart; he would not need to return to Cook County again.

Anne Eastman was headed his way. Kimble gave her a nod and attempted to move past her, but she stopped, hands on hips, blocking his way.

"Do you have a particular interest in our patients' X rays?" she demanded, her tone one of curiosity mixed with indignation.

Kimble felt a cold chill, but did nothing to give himself away. "What do you mean?"

She made a small sound of disbelief as she took a

step nearer. Kimble mirrored her movement, taking a step backwards. "Come on. I saw you looking at that boy's chest film."

Kimble faltered, unable to think of an excuse. "It's a hobby of mine—" He eyed the exit.

Her features twisted with wry disbelief. "What other hobbies do you have? Brain surgery?"

She kept coming; he took another step back and asked, "What do you want?"

She tilted her chin up and looked hard into his eyes. "I want to know how that kid ended up in surgery."

"I'm a janitor," Kimble said weakly. "I did what I was told."

"Bullshit. Who changed those orders?"

Kimble stared at her without answering, but he saw the shift in her expression—confusion, quickly followed by suspicion—as she realized his silence was a confession.

She reached forward and yanked his I.D. from his collar. "You stand right here. I'm calling security."

He bolted for the exit, and did not glance over his shoulder until he reached the double doors leading to the E.R. exit. Only then did he see that she did not follow, but stood staring after him with a perplexed expression.

That night, Gerard lay sleepless, staring at the mental image on his bedroom ceiling of the situation board, which now showed areas of downtown Chicago, with red pins stuck in the locations Richard

Kimble had appeared. At the moment, there were only two—the train station, and Dr. Nichols's racquet club near the Loop.

Not enough to go on. Not yet. But Gerard had a hunch, and his hunches rarely turned out to be wrong. It had to do with the fact that Richard Kimble had returned to Chicago—which made absolutely no sense. If Kimble had escaped with the intent of running, he would have gone someplace very far from here. He would not have returned to his old stomping ground, the place where he was most likely to be recognized.

He either had to be insane, or he had a reason. And Gerard had looked into the depths of Richard Kimble's eyes. The man was desperate, obsessed, but he wasn't crazy. He had returned to Chicago for a reason—and Gerard believed it was to track down the one-armed man.

Of course, the next obvious question was, why? There were two answers to that one, and at the moment, Gerard vacillated wildly as to which one he believed. The first: that Richard Kimble was innocent and wanted to get enough evidence to convict the right man.

The second was more sinister, and yet more believable to Gerard; it presumed that Kimble was guilty, that he had hired the one-armed man to kill his wife, resented the fact that the man walked while Kimble took the rap alone—and so Kimble had come to Chicago to get even one way or another.

He made a mental note to tell Poole to coordinate with Biggs, Newman, and Renfro on a search of all area hospital records and doctor's offices. If the man had a prosthetic limb, he had to have been fitted for it somewhere; there had to be hospital records.

Assuming, of course, that he got the limb in Chicago. Gerard sighed and ran a hand across burning eyes. It was the proverbial needle in the haystack; no wonder Kimble's attorneys had despaired of finding the allegedly homicidal one-armed man. The information was too scanty to be of much use: Male. Caucasian. Early middle age—thirty-five to forty-five. According to Kimble's story, the phony arm had come off just above the elbow.

Without another way to limit the search, trying to get to Kimble via the one-armed man was going to take forever. By the time they found the guy, Kimble would have killed him already and been a continent or two away.

Scratch that plan of attack.

Gerard sighed and drifted off to sleep.

The phone rang in his darkened bedroom sometime after midnight. He picked it up, croaked "Gerard," and cleared his throat.

Renfro's voice was offensively cheerful. "Ever heard of Twenty-three Indole Circle, Inspector?"

Gerard rolled onto his back and closed his eyes as he massaged the bridge of his nose. "Yeah. Lovely place. Had tea there last week." He paused; the sarcasm dropped from his tone. "This had better be good."

"It's Richard Kimble's address."

Gerard sat bolt upright.

"It was a beautiful coincidence," Renfro continued. "Seems Kimble's landlady's grandson was busted for dealing acid. When they took the kid down to the station, he nearly wet himself when he saw Kimble's wanted poster . . ."

But Gerard was listening to none of it. He had already thrown back the sheets, tossed the receiver aside, and was pulling on his pants in the closet.

Within the hour, Gerard descended the stairs and met Renfro inside the basement apartment. Newman stood nearby, peering at photographs and file folders scattered over a narrow, unmade cot while a forensics tech dusted them for prints.

Renfro was smiling. "I can already tell you whose prints we're going to find. Spoke with the landlady and got an affirmative I.D. She says it was Kimble, all right. That makes two eyewitnesses."

Gerard took in the dingy basement with a sweeping gaze—which didn't take much effort. The furnishings consisted of a rust-stained sink and toilet inside a closet-sized bathroom, a rickety table that served as a nightstand, a small, lumpy cot. Gerard moved over to the cot to take a closer look at the files and pictures scattered there. Newman stepped aside to give him a better look.

Gerard gave the younger man a nod. "How's the ear?"

He fancied he could see Newman's pupils contract at the sight of him. "Fine," Newman said shortly, barely gracing his boss with a fleeting sidewise glance. Invisible walls went up around him—which

suited Gerard just fine. Newman would need those
walls if he was to survive in this business; it was the
point of all the hazing. Gerard's superiors had done
no less for him some twenty-odd years ago.

Gerard leaned over to inspect the documents. The
photographs were of artificial limbs—all arms, most
of them extending beyond the elbow joint. He felt a
surge of satisfaction; he had been right. Kimble had
come home to search for the one-armed man. And
his search was about to lead the U.S. marshals to
him.

Gerard reached toward a file folder, hesitated, and
glanced over at the forensics tech, who had just finished with the cot and was straightening.

The tech gave a nod. "Go ahead. Just don't mess
up what we've got, okay?"

Gerard picked up the folder by the edges, opened
it, looked for a clue as to its origin. It contained a
photograph of a fitted prosthetic, clinician's notes of
the fitting.

Beside him, Newman said, "We already sneaked a
peek in most of these. They don't contain the name
of the clinic or hospital."

Gerard scowled as he leafed through the folder.
This apparently wasn't even a patient file, but some
sort of record kept to aid those who designed and
fitted the prosthetics. There were no patient data, no
names or addresses, no notes on follow-up visits. The
only useful bit of information consisted of patients'
surnames jotted on the backs of the photographs.

He wondered whether Kimble had grabbed the
files quickly, fearful of being discovered, then

brought them here and been disappointed . . . Or had he been looking for something other than a name?

"Then we'll go through them all," Gerard said, trying to hide his aggravation that they had come so close to Kimble without advancing the investigation any further. "And we'll use the surnames as our starting point . . ."

He closed the folder and set it carefully back where it had been on the bed.

In the meantime, Newman had been carefully fingering through a stack of files on the bed, checking to be sure all contained the same type of information. Gerard straightened and watched as Newman got to the end of the stack—and found a folded piece of paper lying underneath, directly atop the blanket.

"Have you dusted this?" Newman called to the departing technician, but Gerard had already picked it up and unfolded it to read:

COOK COUNTY MEDICAL
PUBLIC HEALTH SEMINARS

January Is Women's Health Care Month!

Kimble took the el back from the hospital and walked the remaining blocks to the small apartment, trying to decide what to do. It would no longer be safe to return to Cook County—not if Anne Eastman reported him, as she was sure to do. He had wanted to return the folders to the Clinic—the technicians and patients needed the information—but he could no longer risk it. If he had time, perhaps he could mail them.

Collar turned up against the wind and cold, he veered left onto Indole Circle, making his way carefully over the icy sidewalk. Less than half a block away, he stopped, warned by an atavistic intuition of danger.

Two American-made late-model sedans were parked against the curb in front of his apartment building. Light from his basement window streamed out onto the sidewalk and reflected, glittering, off glass windshields, chrome, and ice.

Kimble's breath quickened, filling the cold air with mist. He knew beyond question that these were unmarked cars, that one of them had been driven by Inspector Gerard. But he could not understand how they had traced him here: Anne Eastman had not had his address.

And then it struck him: This had nothing to do with Eastman or the hospital. This had to do with the kid's arrest that afternoon. They had taken him down to the station, where Kimble's photo had been plastered all over the walls . . .

He turned and ran into the night.

The next morning, Gerard walked through the corridors of Cook County Medical, accompanied by Renfro, Biggs, and Poole, and thinking of how Kimble had walked these halls less than twelve hours before.

The three deputies hovered around an E.R. orderly, who was nodding vigorously at Kimble's booking photo, held in Renfro's outstretched hand, while Gerard interrogated the doctor who had been in charge of the E.R. last night, Anne Eastman. Eastman was young, overworked, and completely uncowed by The Look. Gerard liked her immediately. Still, he did not let her off easily.

He frowned at the hospital I.D. in his hand. The name read "Desmondo Jose Ruiz," but the face was Richard Kimble's. "A man posing as a janitor orders an emergency operation and all you do is pull his I.D.?"

He looked back up to see Eastman returning the scowl. Clearly, she considered Gerard an annoyance, a distraction from far more important work. "A little boy's alive today because he did something," she said firmly. Yet another Richard Kimble fan.

Gerard wondered whether she had had time to get to know Kimble well; she was young, attractive, and Kimble was no doubt very lonely. Her gaze was direct, unflinching, honest. Still, Gerard watched her eyes carefully as he said, "So, you weren't aware that when he escaped, he was being transported to Menard State Prison to begin a walk down death row . . . ?"

Eastman drew back slightly, gasping. Her horror pleased Gerard.

"He murdered his wife," Gerard replied. At Eastman's unfeigned surprise, he almost smiled. He did not expect she would be doing anything to help Kimble in the near future.

"Thank you for your help, Doctor," he said politely, and moved over to where Kimble had been the night before with the kid's gurney. He visualized Kimble there, in his janitor's uniform, slipping through the chaos without arousing attention. He could *see* him, almost smell him, and felt a keen sense of frustration that he could not simply reach across the span of hours and touch him.

And in his mind's eye, he saw Kimble rolling the gurney down the hallway, and looking down at the sight of a young kid, moaning and in serious pain. And the surgeon's eyes had clouded, with that look that—

Gerard censored the stray thought immediately.

Renfro finished up his questioning of the orderly, and he and the other deputies convened around Gerard.

Renfro was shaking his head. "What I can't figure is, if you were Kimble, why would you take a major-league chance of hanging around a trauma ward? The place is crawling with cops."

"He's a thrill junkie," Poole suggested scornfully.

Biggs's expression grew thoughtful. "Or maybe his wound was more serious than we thought. Or maybe it got infected, and he had to have more supplies . . ."

"Still doesn't explain why he would take the time to help the kid," Renfro said.

Gerard ignored them as a middle-aged man passed by. Something about the man's posture, his bearing, caught Gerard's attention; he narrowed his eyes, began to walk behind the man down the hall.

It was the arm—the left arm, below the elbow. It hung at a slightly unnatural angle, and as Gerard neared, he realized that the color of the hand peeking out below the man's sleeve did not quite match the rest of the man's skin tone.

He followed as the man turned and walked down the corridor, away from the emergency room. The hall cornered abruptly to the right. As the man rounded another corner and came to a set of glass double doors, he sensed someone tailing him, and came to a halt.

He held the door open and faced Gerard. "Can I help you find something?"

Gerard smiled, looking past the man to the corridor beyond, and a second door marked "PROSTHETIC CLINIC."

"Thank you, sir," he said, with utter sincerity. "I think you already have."

At that same time, Kimble was doing some investigating of his own. He had spent the night in a cheap hotel, then wandered in the run-down neighborhood until he found a bar that filled his criteria: it had a pay phone, it wasn't crowded (there was one alkie at the scarred oak bar, drinking with quiet, methodical efficiency), and it was open at nine A.M. Kimble wandered through the faint haze of smoke, which writhed serpentlike in the pane of sunlight filtering through the open door, bought a beer at the bar and left it untouched on the counter, then headed toward the back. In the dark, narrow rest-room corridor which stank of urine and stale cigarettes, he found the pay phone. This time, luck was with him; there was a greater Chicago area telephone book, and he found likely numbers for four of the names. The fifth he got from information.

He began making calls. He found three possible listings for the first name on his list, Raymond Johnston: an R. A. Johnston, an R. J. Johnston, and a Ray. No Raymond listed. He called all three. R. A. was a Robert, and R. J. wouldn't give his name, but wanted to know who the hell this Raymond was. With the third, Ray Johnston's wife answered, and Kimble launched into his cover spiel:

"Yes . . . This is Dr. Elway at Cook County. I'm doing follow-up work for the Prosthetic Clinic for Raymond Johnston. . . . Do I have the right man?"

"Yes," the woman said dully. "Ray's asleep with the flu. Whaddya want to know?"

"I simply wanted to ask him a few questions about how his prosthesis was working."

"They're doing fine," the woman said. "Though Ray says sometimes the right one goes a little wonky on him."

Kimble hesitated. "The right one?"

"Yeah. Left arm works just fine. He gets around good with it. Half the time, people don't even know."

Kimble instructed her to have Ray contact the clinic if he had any more problems with the right arm, and hung up.

Scratch one.

He dialed the one number he'd gotten from information for the second name, Costas Milkis. No question about that one being the right one. Milkis, however, was chronically ill and had been confined to a wheelchair for the past year and a half. Scratch two.

The third, Matthew Zelick, had died. Kimble apologized to the grieving spouse, then hung up the telephone and crossed the third one off his list. He stared at the two names remaining: Clive Driscoll and Frederick Sykes. One of them had to be the man who had killed Helen. Kimble studied them both, tried to decide which name looked more like a killer's.

He drew a breath and dialed Driscoll's number. A man answered.

"Yes," Kimble said, trying to keep the surge of adrenaline from showing in his voice. "I'm looking for Clive Driscoll . . ."

"Clive ain't here," the man said suspiciously. "This is Jesse. His brother. Who's this?"

Kimble affected a heartily cheerful tone. "This is Ted Riley with the high school reunion committee. Believe it or not, twenty-five years is just around the corner, and Clive's on our list of lost souls . . ."

"Clive's in jail. Cops say he tried to hold up a savings and loan."

Kimble flashed on a memory: Slamming his bedroom door against the intruder, seeing gleaming metal fall, clatter against the floor. Diving after the gun—

He forced a laugh. "No kidding? Armed robbery? He's where?"

"The federal lockup. You know the one, near the train station downtown . . ."

"Yeah," Kimble replied, with no small amount of irony. "Yeah, I know the one . . . Thanks."

He dialed Sykes's number next. It rang off the hook. The man had probably already left for work.

Kimble replaced the receiver in the cradle and stared down at the list in his hands with a sense of growing dread.

Driscoll was the killer. *Had* to be, and yet Kimble did not want to admit it to himself. Because if Driscoll was the killer, there was only one way to get to him, and that way was almost certain to get Kimble captured or killed.

At the same time, he knew he had no choice. With a sense of growing dread, he pocketed the list of names and went out, squinting at the bright sunlight.

9

Gerard stood beside the computer inside the Prosthetic Clinic while Renfro and Poole watched, impressed, as a technician fitted a special demonstration prosthesis on Biggs. The clinic was a busy, fascinating place, but Gerard paid only cursory attention to the technicians fitting and testing limbs, to Biggs's delight as he flexed a muscle in his shoulder and watched the artificial hand curl in response.

At the moment, Gerard was far too preoccupied to delight in the wonders of science; his hunch had proved correct. The one-armed man existed, and Kimble was trying to find him. Which meant that Gerard's theory that Kimble was an angry dupe of a professional killer had merit, too.

Either way, Gerard wanted to be sure to get there first. But he could not help being distracted by the fact that the one-armed man had not simply been the product of a desperate killer's imagination. Kimble had been telling the truth—about the man's existence, at least.

The director of the clinic stood beside him, watching with pride as Biggs flexed the artificial hand. She looked like all the others working there—pale, bespectacled, with a round, soft body and an air of deep contentment that came from being paid for doing what she loved most. She seemed far more interested in giving a tour of the place than in answering Gerard's questions.

"Tell me again about how we might go about locating a suspect," Gerard repeated.

The director turned toward him and blinked behind her thick-lensed spectacles. "Oh," she said, and from her intonation, it was clear she had entirely forgotten what she had just been talking about. She glanced down at the computer, where a white-smocked technician sat, awaiting instructions. "The files are very straightforward if you know the parameters of the person you're looking for."

Gerard squinted at the computer screen. Nothing on it looked very straightforward to him.

Before facing the monitor, the tech at the computer smiled up at him, with a look acknowledging that the director was a total flake. The director, of course, completely missed the look.

The technician played the keyboard with startling speed, then blinked at the results on the flashing screen. "You have an initial pool of three hundred twenty-five white males."

Gerard called over to Poole, who was running her fingers over the demo prosthesis attached to Biggs's arm, and murmuring something about realism. "Poole," he snapped, and she glanced up, instantly alert at the sound of her name. "Give me Kimble's account on the night of the murder."

Poole slipped the file out of her over-the-shoulder briefcase and rifled through it.

"The one-armed man," Gerard prompted. "Missing the right or left hand?"

Poole scanned, and did not look up as she answered, "Right."

The tech entered the information. The monitor screen flashed briefly, then a number appeared on the screen: 250.

"Age thirty-five to forty-five," Poole read.

The tech's fingers played a lightning-swift allegro on the keys. The screen flashed, and the number dropped to 117.

"Living in the greater Chicago area," Gerard added.

Fifty-three.

Gerard stared at the number, thinking.

The computer tech looked up at him. "Do you have the location of the attachment?"

"Funny bone," Gerard replied.

At the tech's puzzled expression, Poole translated. "Mid-humerus."

Twenty.

"It could take us a week to track down every one of those names," Renfro complained, and fell silent as Gerard shot him a look that said he did not need to hear the obvious.

Gerard picked up the nearest phone without asking, punched a free line, and dialed a number. When the party answered, he said, "Stevens. I've got a list of names I want searched for criminal history."

Kimble stood on the sidewalk and stared at the imposing gray stone edifice across the noisy, traffic-filled street. The very sight of it triggered a heart-pounding physical reaction that verged on nausea; he fought to slow his breathing.

On the way here, he had stopped twice at telephone kiosks, hoping to make contact with the fifth man on the list, Frederick Sykes, but there was still no answer at Sykes's number.

No putting it off. Gerard could be on his trail at this very moment; he might as well take his chances and see Clive Driscoll face-to-face.

As the light changed and the "WALK" signal began to flash, Kimble drew a deep breath and crossed the street. As he entered the revolving glass door that led into the lobby of the federal jail, he made himself a firm promise: If they recognized him before he saw Driscoll and was able to identify him as Helen's killer, he would run, even if it meant being shot in the back. That at least would be a quicker fate than the prolonged walk down death row that awaited him if he was recaptured.

And if he *did* recognize Driscoll . . .

The thought of having to stare into the eyes of his

wife's murderer again added to the intensity of Kimble's anxiety. He was not at all sure what he would do, what he would say; he was not sure he would be able to keep from flinging himself in a mindless rage at the bars.

He would have to. He had no evidence against him; not yet. He had to get his hands on *something* before he dared go to the police.

Kimble paused in the lobby and tried not to look too uncomfortable and out of place as he studied the directory by the elevator banks, then pressed the UP button.

One of the elevators opened almost immediately; it contained a half dozen cops who had come up from basement parking. Kimble fought the impulse to run and stood rooted to the spot, staring at the cops, wondering whether it would look too suspicious if he passed up this elevator in favor of another.

It would. There was room for at least another two or three people. One of the cops caught the door and held it for Kimble.

"Comin' or not?"

Kimble forced himself to step into the elevator. He turned immediately and faced the seam in the door, trying to ignore the breath of a dozen cops on his neck, and watching with upturned eyes as the old elevator groaned and began moving upward. The cop beside him gave him the once-over, then turned away, yawning.

The elevator rose at a maddeningly languid pace. Kimble counted the floors as the indicator light moved up, up, finally coming to the floor before his . . .

And then, just before it reached his destination, the elevator slid to a full stop between floors. The overhead lights flickered. Kimble bowed his head and tried not to tremble visibly.

"Aw, shit . . ." one of the cops behind him groaned. "Not now . . ."

"Anybody bring a pack of cards?" another joked.

The elevator restarted with an abrupt lurch; a muted bell rang as it stopped at the fifth floor. The doors opened, and Kimble stepped out into the visitation area and breathed in a smell he had come to despise: sweat, metal, and despair, combined with the faint aroma of singed cotton from the prison laundry and canned stewed tomatoes from the kitchen.

He stepped up behind another visitor, a teary-eyed young woman who stood clutching a crumpled tissue at the clearing officer's desk. "Booth Three," the officer droned, in a tone unutterably bored and uninflected, as though he had memorized the words without having the faintest clue as to their meaning. "No hands on the glass. Five minutes maximum. Be advised that under a federal court ruling your conversation can be recorded. Next."

He said the last word so swiftly and without a break that the tearful young woman hesitated an instant, uncertain as to whether she had been dismissed. And then she turned to her right and headed for the partitioned booths, marked overhead with numbers.

Kimble stepped up immediately to the counter.

The officer studied a wart on his middle finger as he said, "Name of inmate?" It sounded like a tonelessly flat statement of fact, but Kimble was used to it. He replied quickly,

"Clive Driscoll."

Still without looking up at him, the officer spun his clipboard around. "Sign here, print your name, address, and relationship to inmate below." He leaned forward, and in exactly the same voice said, "Two-zero-ten. Driscoll, Clive R."

In the box that said "Name," Kimble carefully printed "Jesse Pulver," along with the address he'd found in the telephone book. On the line marked "Relationship," he wrote "Friend," then slid the clipboard back at the clearing officer.

The officer glanced over the information, then went back to picking at the wart. "Be about five minutes. You can wait in the hall."

He nodded at the row of chairs lining the far wall.

Kimble sat on a torn faux-leather chair with broken springs and ducked his head each time someone passed by. After a nerve-racking six minutes during which he was several times tempted to leap to his feet and run out of the building, the clearing officer leaned over his counter and looked at him.

"Visitor for Driscoll . . . ?"

Kimble was on his feet.

"Booth Seven," he said. "No hands on the glass. Be advised . . ."

Kimble did not stay to hear the rest of it. He strode down the row of chairs and rounded the last partition to Booth Seven, all the while holding the image of Helen's killer—

olive-skinned, with dark, curling hair, dark eyes, wheeling toward him with surprise and anger etched over thick, homely features, reaching for the detached arm—

in his mind. At the last instant, Kimble took a breath, held it, and stepped forward, eyes ablaze, to face Driscoll.

And sagged as he released the breath. Driscoll was a small, wiry black man with restless light brown eyes. He sat with hands—one real, one artificial— clasped on his side of the counter and looked across the glass-and-metal barrier at Kimble. "So who're you?"

The wrong man. Kimble recoiled. He had risked everything by coming here, for the *wrong man*. He wanted desperately, frantically to be gone, to be far, far away from Driscoll, from the smell of this place.

"Doesn't matter," he mumbled. "I made a mistake."

Hope and loneliness replaced the suspicion in Driscoll's eyes. "Shit, that's okay. Stick around a few minutes, talk about whatever you want . . ."

But Kimble had already begun striding down the long hallway. He walked out of the visitation area to the elevator bank, where another crowd of cops lingered.

He wheeled, and headed to the end of the corridor, for the door marked STAIRS.

* * *

A few phone calls pared Gerard's list of twenty down to six almost immediately; he gave Poole and Renfro three, while he and Biggs took the three others. Of course, he checked out Driscoll first. The fact that the guy was awaiting trial for armed robbery made him the most likely of all the suspects.

Accompanied by Biggs, Gerard crossed the main-floor lobby of the federal lockup and flashed his U.S. marshal's I.D. at the desk clerk. "We need to see a prisoner."

She jerked with her chin at a nearby bank of elevators. "Fifth floor."

The two men moved over to the elevators; the indicator lights had all frozen at upper levels. The closest was the eleventh floor.

"It's hinky," Biggs said thoughtfully, as he and Gerard stared up the lights. One of them eased down to the ninth floor, and stayed there. "Man risks everything to find a one-armed man his investigators couldn't find in pretrial investigation. Something's really hinky about this thing." He looked over at Gerard and watched carefully for a reaction.

Gerard did not give him one. He knew that Biggs and the others were just now beginning to consider that Kimble might have been telling the truth, but Gerard could not face that fact.

Hinky.

Gerard's upper lip twitched ever so slightly with scorn; slowly, he turned his face toward Biggs's. "I hate that word."

Biggs looked quickly away, up at the indicator lights, but there was a gleam of disbelief in his eye that irritated Gerard. He jabbed the UP button again, paced in place a bit, then swore softly.

"Where're the damn stairs?"

Biggs was aghast. "It's five flights!"

Gerard looked his cohort's brawny build up and down with contempt. "Then you wait."

Without looking to see if Biggs followed, he headed for the door marked STAIRS and started up.

Out of impatience, he half ran. At the third-floor landing, he leaned over the railing to stare down at the people moving down the spiraling stairwell floors below. Evidently Biggs had chosen to wait for the elevator. Gerard continued on, dashing up a fourth flight, skimming shoulders at the outset with another man headed down and just stepping onto the third-floor landing.

A dark-haired man, wearing nondescript street clothing. His head was down, and Gerard did not catch sight of his face, but as he made it onto the fourth-floor landing, Gerard stopped short, alerted by something he sensed but could not explain. Poole would have said that he smelled his prey.

Gerard leaned suddenly over the railing to watch the dark-haired man moving in a swift downward spiral below. It could have been anyone; Gerard instinctively knew it was not. As a test, he called down, his voice echoing down the stairwell:

"Kimble!"

The others on the stairs glanced up out of curiosity—all except the dark-haired man. He faltered, almost lost his balance, then recovered and increased his pace.

The misstep confirmed what Gerard already knew; he drew his weapon and hurtled down the stairs. *"Kimble!"*

The man broke into an all-out run. Gerard tried to get a bead, couldn't, and wheeled around, heading for the landing door. It swung open, almost striking him in the face, and he collided head-on with a Chicago cop.

Gerard gripped the cop by the shoulders, shouted in his face. "U.S. marshal! Get on the phone, call your commander! Tell him there's a top-fifteen warrant in this building. *Go!*" He twirled the dazed cop around, shoved him back toward the landing door, and started running down the stairs again, leaping down them two at a time.

By the time he pushed through the fire door to the main-floor lobby, Kimble's breath was coming in shallow, ragged sobs. He had never been this frightened, not when he had been trapped in the wrecked bus and seen the light of the oncoming train, not when he had stood staring down at the roaring Barkley Dam falls with Inspector Gerard's pistol pointed at his back—never, because he had never before been this close to finding Helen's killer. That one sound— his name, on Gerard's lips—had struck more fear in him than the deafening scream of the train's screaming brakes. Certainly Gerard seemed more relentless, more immovable than any locomotive.

But he could not die now, not when he was so close.

As he fled into the lobby, two uniformed police officers standing near the doors looked up, drew their weapons, began to move toward him.

In a burst of inspiration, Kimble gasped, "Officers! There's a man in the stairwell waving a gun and screaming!"

The cops bought it, yanked open the doors, pounded up the stairs.

Kimble slowed, did not allow himself to run, but moved swiftly around clusters of pedestrians. The glass doors were not that far; Gerard had been at least two flights behind him, and the cops would slow him for at least an extra few seconds. If Kimble could just get to the street, he could make it . . .

An eardrum-shattering klaxon began to blare.

The pedestrians around Kimble stopped. The civilians gazed around in confusion, looking for the cause; the cops all knew what was happening and began to draw their weapons.

Kimble broke into a dead run. To his horror, the exit in front of him began to swing slowly shut. He sprinted and did a home-plate slide into it, jamming his hard-soled shoe into the narrowing gap and bracing it open. He would have made it out then, but a large man entering from the outside realized that Kimble was fleeing, and yanked on the door, trapping him inside.

Around them, other doors snapped shut and sealed with an electric buzz.

Kimble pulled himself up and shoved the entire width of his foot into the door. The large man resisted, but the crack slowly widened as Kimble pushed. He slipped a hand through, and then an arm to the elbow, then a calf, and the rest of a leg to the hip . . .

He jerked his head as Gerard's voice came behind him, cutting through the nerve-jangling screech of the klaxon:

"Down, down, everybody down!"

The large man dropped for the sidewalk, leaving Kimble to wrestle against the electronic lock on his own. The motor growled as the door strained to close on Kimble's leg. He watched in horror as civilians dove for the marble floor; bodies fell away until a lone figure remained standing in the lobby.

Not my problem . . .

With impossible effort, Kimble squeezed bone and flesh through a place too narrow for them to fit, wriggling until he emerged outside, free. He lunged forward—

And fell. The door had latched on to his foot, crushing it like a bear trap. He struggled up onto one leg, straining forward, gritting his teeth with pain and effort, and twisted back to peer over his shoulder at his pursuer.

Gerard was charging the glass doors, gun leveled straight at Kimble's face.

Kimble flailed, hunched forward, and clawed the sidewalk, making the muted, desperate sounds of a trapped animal, one eye on his goal, the other on Gerard.

Behind the glass doors, Gerard knelt in shooter's stance. He was close enough to his target to lock gazes with him, close enough to kill, and in his eyes

Kimble saw a horrifying mixture of cold dutifulness and regret.

Not my problem . . .

The klaxon ceased abruptly. Kimble turned and clawed the ground, seeing nothing now except blood-red frustration, and, encroaching on its borders, consuming all else, white swirls of snow.

Gerard fired, seven times in two seconds. Kimble dropped before the first shot.

Civilians screamed. Their cries along with the sound of gunfire echoed for seconds; and then the lobby fell deathly silent.

Gerard rose and stepped to the door. On the other side of cratered glass, Richard Kimble rose on shaking legs and stared back at him, stunned. For one frozen instant they beheld each other; Gerard lifted a hand wonderingly to a bullet hole shattered in the glass.

Abruptly, Kimble came to himself. With a strength born of adrenaline, he yanked his foot free. The door moaned shut as he dashed into traffic.

On the other side of the pockmarked glass, Gerard watched as Kimble made it safely across the street and disappeared into a crowd of pedestrians. He lifted a hand and began to pound in frustration against the heavy glass. "Open the doors!"

Biggs came up behind, weapon in his hand. Gerard stepped back beside him, staring across the street in the direction where Kimble had vanished. His sole came down on something hard, irregularly shaped;

he bent down to retrieve it, and picked up a flattened slug. Six others lay scattered on the polished floor.

"Bulletproof glass," Biggs said unnecessarily. Gerard simply gazed at him.

The glass doors buzzed, causing Biggs to start. Gerard watched as they swung slowly open onto the bustling sidewalk, his prey nowhere in sight.

Kimble let the adrenaline propel him across town, toward the address given in the telephone directory for Frederick Sykes. He found the apartment house—an older, two-story brick building, with separate apartment entrances all facing the street. Kimble crossed to the other side, went into a pizza parlor that looked onto the building, and stood watching Sykes's apartment door as he dialed up the phone number.

He let it ring ten times, then hung up and headed for the door of the pizza parlor, pausing at the plate-glass window to scope out the street.

It seemed empty, and Kimble moved out onto the sidewalk—and stopped as he saw a man, a covered Styrofoam cup in each hand, approach a car parked nearby. The woman inside leaned across the seat and opened the door. The man handed her a cup and started to climb in—but paused first to shift something on his hip.

A gun. The man got inside the car, slammed the door, and the two of them sipped coffee, their gazes never wavering from the door of Sykes's apartment.

Kimble turned and headed out the back of the shop. In one way, the sight of cops was encouraging;

it meant Sykes was under suspicion. Perhaps even Gerard himself had ordered the watch, which meant that he had come to believe in the existence of the one-armed man . . .

Kimble's lips thinned. Impossible; a couple of hours ago, Gerard had tried to gun him down, which simply meant that he knew the one-armed man was involved, but not how.

One cold, hard son of a bitch. But he was Kimble's last chance. Gerard was relentless; and if he became convinced of Kimble's innocence, he would never rest until he saw justice done.

But Kimble had the feeling he was going to prove damnably hard to convince.

He moved through the alleyway behind the row of shops, and went the long way around to the rear of the apartment building. From there he crawled up the fire escape to Sykes's apartment—not an easy task, as the escape ended ten feet above the ground, and Kimble had to crawl up a window ledge, jump for the last metal rung, then swing himself up chin-up style. He used what he could of the remaining adrenaline in his system, which wasn't much; he was deeply exhausted from lack of sleep and the physical exertion of the last two days. The struggle to free himself from the glass door seemed to have pulled every muscle in his body. But the realization that Sykes was the last suspect on his list propelled him onward.

If Sykes was not the right man—

Kimble did not permit himself to consider the possibility. On the metal-grate landing behind Sykes's apartment, he cupped a hand over his eyebrows and peered into the apartment.

No lights, no sign of anyone home. The kitchen was dark, empty; dirty dishes lay heaped in the sink.

Kimble knocked on the back door and waited half a minute, then knocked again. Still no answer. He took a step back, glancing over both shoulders to ensure that the alleyway was empty, then hoisted back his fist and jammed it against the glass window.

It cracked. A jagged section fell out, one piece tinkling as it fell through the metal escape by Kimble's feet down into the alleyway below. A few pieces fell inward and shattered on the kitchen floor.

Kimble reached in, unlocked the door, and moved swiftly into the kitchen, closing the door behind him. Crime number seven: breaking and entering.

The apartment was dark, silent. He headed into the living room, modest by his standards of a year ago, a palace by his current. No fireplace, just worn, comfortable furniture: a camelback sofa with a folded comforter hung over its back, an overstuffed, sagging recliner, a small television on a pressboard stand.

Kimble paused at an end table beside the recliner to look at a group of framed photographs: a teenaged girl in a cheerleading outfit, a grinning boy in a football uniform. The sight of them convinced Kimble at once that he had the wrong man; this man was a father, with a family. This man could not possibly kill . . .

And then he picked up the photo of a thirtyish man dressed in a Chicago Police Department uniform. The picture was obviously posed; the man stood stiffly, hands clasped awkwardly in front of him, but he did not smile because the flash had caught him off guard. He faced the photographer with a look of startled surprise in his wide, dark eyes.

The same look he had worn that night in Kimble's townhouse, when his artificial limb had been torn from him.

10

Kimble set down the photograph with trembling hands and a sense of triumph blended with horror. The man in the photograph had the same face, the same build, the same dark eyes, and dark, curly hair that Kimble remembered.

At last, he had found his wife's killer: Frederick Sykes. Now all he had to do was locate some shred of evidence linking Sykes to Helen's murder. But what? He had not thought beyond this moment; perhaps he had secretly believed he would never get this far.

He hesitated then, and glanced back at the photograph in his hands. The man in the picture—no doubt Sykes—was able-bodied, not wearing a prosthesis. But the photo looked at least ten years old. It was possible Sykes had suffered some sort of accident which caused him to lose an arm and retire from the force.

Or could it be that he, Kimble, was so desperate to find his wife's killer that he felt so certain of Sykes's guilt? He had only seen the man in dim lighting, for a few seconds during a struggle that occurred a year ago . . .

Without knowing what he was searching for, Kimble set down the photograph and moved through the short hallway that led to the single small bedroom. It was Spartan: a desk, an unadorned dresser, one twin bed with a single pillow. Whatever previous relationships he had had, Sykes lived alone now. Kimble opened the closet, the dresser. In the bottom drawer, as he rifled through folded shirts and jeans, his hand brushed against something plastic, resilient, cool.

(nonliving skin beneath his fingers, the feel of resistance as he pulled, then twisted . . .)

He pulled out a prosthetic arm, most of it worn with time and slightly discolored. But one section seemed new, fresh. Repaired.

Kimble sat down heavily in the chair in front of the small desk and wept soundlessly.

When he recovered, he started going through the desk drawers. There were boxes of pencils, paper clips, rubber bands, a folder full of financial documents, but what sparked Kimble's interest were a couple of packages of photographs. He pulled them out and started looking at them.

There were more pictures of the kids—it looked as if the boy had married, and there were pictures of a grandbaby. But what interested Kimble most were pictures taken of Sykes on what appeared to be a company vacation junket. He flipped through them, noticing one of Sykes standing beside a large fish—and then he stopped. Paused. Thumbed back to the photograph.

In the photo, Sykes and another man stood smiling on either side of a large sport fish hung from the dock. It was the face of the second man—younger, better dressed than Sykes—that had caused Kimble to stop in his tracks; a vaguely familiar face, and Kimble struggled for the space of a minute trying to place it.

He closed his eyes, scanning his memory until at last he heard the voice of Charlie Nichols saying, above the noise of the milling crowd: *Richard! I just saw someone who wanted to meet you . . . Richard Kimble . . . Alex Lentz. Alex is working on the RDU90 trials for Devlin-Macgregor.*

Yes. Kimble opened his eyes, stared at the tan, smiling young face as its owner's voice spoke in his memory: *Sorry, we've been trading phone calls the last few days. Something about a biopsy report I returned to you?*

Next image, from that same terrible night: Chief Resident Surgeon Falawi's dark, exhausted eyes above his pale-green mask, glancing up at Kimble as they worked to stop a man from bleeding to death—a man with a badly damaged liver. *He's on a drug protocol. RDU90.*

The hostile look in Alex Lentz's eyes as he stared, thinking himself unseen, at Kimble across the crowded ballroom . . .

Unease settled over Kimble; he felt himself teetering on the precipice of revelation, but he continued going through the desk drawers. From an expanding folder full of bills and receipts, he fished out a stack of paycheck stubs bound by a rubber band. In the top right corner was the Devlin-Macgregor Pharmaceutical logo; beside the net pay amount was typed "Payroll level four: Security."

Kimble sagged in the chair, stunned by a sudden flash of insight.

What if Helen's death had not been a random killing? *What if Helen's death had not been a random killing?* What if Sykes had meant to kill him, too, before he could blow the whistle on RDU90, but the emergency call from Tim Price had saved his life? And if he had not been called away to surgery . . . Kimble covered his face with his hands and thought, *I should have died too . . .*

No. He straightened, lowered his hands. No, it was better to have lived, despite the pain. At least this way Sykes would be brought to justice.

Kimble stared at the payroll stubs for a long time.

And then he went to the kitchen, called information for a number, and dialed it.

By late morning, Gerard was back at the U.S. Marshal's Office, in the kitchenette off the hallway, pouring his sixth cup of coffee as he mentally reviewed the events at the lockup. Driscoll was still the most obvious suspect, especially with his armed robbery record. Kimble had been coming back from a visit with him, but Driscoll claimed he had no clue as to who Kimble was or why he had come to see him. He seemed to be telling the truth—but it was Gerard's experience that hired guns were very good at seeming to be telling the truth.

There were two other likely suspects, and Gerard had both their residences put under surveillance. He was not quite sure what Kimble would do now; it all rode on whether Driscoll was the man. Certainly, Kimble wouldn't be going back to visit the federal lockup anytime soon, even if he badly wanted Driscoll's hide. Perhaps he would simply run.

Gerard was kicking himself now for not shooting Kimble in the foot when he had the chance.

He could hear Renfro talking across the hallway, in Biggs's office. "I agree. This is getting too hinky. I mean, it was nuts for him to walk into the lockup. Absolutely nuts . . ."

Gerard's lip curled at the word *hinky*. He set the coffeepot back on the burner and moved into the hallway, on the verge of calling out something scathing at Renfro. At that second, his secretary, Jenna, stepped in front of him, her face blank with shock.

"It's Kimble on line three," Jenna said.

Gerard allowed himself less than a second's double take. He jerked his head in the direction of Biggs's office and barked: "Renfro! Biggs!"

The two men had heard Jenna's announcement and were already on their way out Biggs's door. They followed Gerard as he ran, mindful of the sloshing Styrofoam cup of coffee, toward the media room.

"He *announced* himself?!" Renfro asked, in a voice full of wonder.

"Got to be a crank," Biggs huffed.

Gerard did not answer. He had already considered the possibility; at the same time, he wasn't about to risk missing out on a conversation with Kimble. He wheeled into the media room, set down the coffee on the table beside the telephone, and nodded to the technician who was already ready and waiting at the control console.

Gerard picked up the receiver, and the trace began.

"This is Gerard."

Kimble wasted no time with introductions. "Do you remember what I told you in the tunnel?"

He drew a deep breath and said calmly, "You told me you didn't kill your wife."

"Remember what you said to me?"

Gerard remembered all too well, but said, "I remember you were pointing my gun at me."

"You said, 'I don't care.' "

Renfro crouched beside the seated technician. From where he stood, Gerard could see a swift-changing readout of digital numbers on the tracing equipment. One suddenly locked on, and the tech excitedly whispered something to Renfro. Gerard strained to hear what she was saying—something about the South Side. He could not fathom why Kimble had called; he had thought the surgeon too shrewd, too wily to do anything as stupid, as pointless as this. This was the act of a madman seeking an audience. Maybe Renfro was right—maybe the man was nuts.

Even so, Gerard played along, speaking slowly, taking his time to reply. The longer he held the surgeon on the line, the better. "That's right, Kimble . . . I'm not trying to solve a puzzle here. Someone else decided whether you were guilty or not. I'm just the poor working man that's paid to hunt you down."

Poole stole into the room, her eyes focused on Gerard's lips, and went to stand beside Biggs. Gerard watched the tech's console as the second digit of the phone number locked in.

"He's in the Pullman area," Renfro said softly. "Fifteen seconds for location."

Kimble did not seem in a hurry to get off the phone. His tone was conversational, unrushed. "Well, I *am* trying to solve the puzzle, Gerard . . . and I just found a piece."

Gerard's eyes widened at this bit of information. Driscoll, he decided, mind racing. He had to be the man. Kimble recognized him this morning, but if that was the case, why hadn't he simply drawn a gun and blown Driscoll away?

Newman came into the room, file in his hand, mouth open to speak; the others turned to him and raised their fingers for silence. He immediately picked up on what was happening and listened along with the others.

"I hope this means you're giving yourself up?" Gerard asked.

Kimble hesitated. For an instant, Gerard feared he would hang up. Surely he realized that the marshal's office was tracing the call and would have the number any second . . .

"It turns out it's not as simple as that." Kimble sounded abruptly bone weary. "Since it's not your job to care about these things, I won't bother you with the details. I just thought I'd let you know I've got some more things to find out."

Gerard didn't buy it for an instant. Kimble wasn't nuts, and he wasn't stupid; he was doing this because he had something up his sleeve. But from his voice, it was clear he was tired, dead tired, and if he kept going much longer he was going to be tired enough to screw up.

With quiet, utter sincerity, Gerard said, "You're running out of time, Kimble. The longer you stay out, the more dangerous it gets."

"Thank you for your concern," Kimble answered faintly. "I must say, this morning you had a hell of an odd way of showing it."

A *bang*. Gerard started, then realized it was the sound of the phone being slammed down.

"You can't control this thing, Kimble. Kimble?"

Silence, but no dial tone. The sound of receding footsteps.

Kimble had walked away and left the receiver off the hook.

Gerard covered the mouthpiece and glanced at Renfro. "Where is he?"

Renfro was staring down at the numbers on the console in unmasked amazement. "Holy shit! We've got a car there right now—!"

* * *

The glass in the rear door to Sykes's apartment had been broken, and Kimble had let himself in. Gerard found the buzzing receiver off the hook where Kimble had left it, on the kitchen counter. Kimble must have anticipated that the cops surveilling the apartment would come rushing in the front, and had slipped out the back and down the fire escape into the alleyway.

Poole followed him in, reading from a file folder. Back in the kitchen and out by the front door, Renfro and a couple of techs were dusting for prints and processing the crime scene. "Name is Frederick Sykes. Forty-five. Ex-cop."

Gerard replaced the receiver in the cradle. One of the forensics techs, a man ten years Gerard's senior, approached. "Inspector, we're ready for you to look at this."

Gerard and Poole followed him back to a small desk. The tech sat, pulled out a set of check stubs, some papers, and a package of photographs. "Kimble's prints are all over the apartment," the tech explained, "but the concentration is here."

He opened the package, slid out the photos, and stopped at one. "He flipped through the pack, but paused here . . ." He handed Gerard the picture.

Gerard stared at it. He saw two men and a fish, and tried to fathom why these would be meaningful to Richard Kimble. He looked down at the tech. "Let me see the negatives."

The tech handed them over. Gerard unscrolled the strip of film, held it to the light, and squinted at it.

"One's missing," he murmured, as much to himself as to the other man.

The radio in his jacket squawked, and Biggs's voice filtered through the grid. "Here he comes . . ."

"We're ready for him," Gerard said. He returned the negatives to the tech, but held on to the photograph.

One minute later, Sykes entered through the front. Gerard slipped the photo into his pocket, and waited with Poole at the kitchen entrance.

Sykes was one armed, all right, but the folks at the Prosthetic Clinic had done such good work it was hard to tell unless you were looking for it. He was a large, coarse-featured man, with curly dark hair, big bones, and a broad build; even so, Biggs, who followed close behind, stood half a head taller. Sykes stood in the doorway gaping for a second, and then he marched inside, all indignation and outrage.

"What the hell's going on here? Who are you people?"

Gerard stepped forward and met him with The Look. "You had a break-in, Mister Sykes."

Sykes glared at him, clenched his fists as if ready for a fight. There was a hardness to him that Gerard had seen in many a booking photo, and it made him suddenly sorry that Sykes had ever been on the Chicago Police Force. "Yeah?" Sykes snarled. "You a cop?"

"My name is Gerard. U.S. Marshal's Office."

The statement had the desired effect. Sykes blanched, took a confused step backward, all the fight drained from him.

"This morning a fugitive named Richard Kimble made a call from your apartment," Gerard said.

Sykes blinked, dazed. "Richard Kimble? I don't know any Richard Kimble."

Convincing, but not quite so much as Driscoll had been. Poole produced a photograph from one of her files and thrust it at Sykes.

Sykes bit his lower lip, his bushy eyebrows knit in concentration as he contemplated the picture. "Wait a minute . . . This is the doctor who killed his wife. . . . He claimed the killer had a prosthetic limb. You telling me he's coming after me?" A glimmer of fear shone in Sykes's dark eyes.

Gerard didn't buy the act for an instant. He knew, with the inexpressible certainty born of intuition, that Sykes was guilty, Sykes was involved. He stared at the ex-cop with growing hate, yet he kept his tone flat, polite, inscrutable. "Would he have a reason to?"

Sykes looked up at him swiftly. "What the hell's that supposed to mean? Because I have this?" He lifted his prosthetic arm. "Look, a year ago some people came to see me. They asked me questions about the night of the murder and I'll tell you the same thing I told them." His tone grew indignant, angry again. "I wasn't even *in* town that night. I was on a business trip."

Gerard nodded and moved out into the living room, picked up the photographs on the end table, studied them. Sykes and Poole followed. Gerard studied the photograph of an able-bodied Sykes dressed in a police uniform, and turned. "What kind of business are you in, Mr. Sykes?"

"Security."

"Independent?"

Sykes shook his head, keeping his gaze fastened on Gerard's every move. "No. I work for a pharmaceutical company. I handle security for its top executives."

Gerard pulled from his pocket the photograph of Sykes with another man and the trophy fish, and held it up for Sykes to see. "Any idea why Kimble would be interested in these?" He focused intently on the one-armed man's eyes.

Sykes began blinking rapidly. Began lying, Gerard knew. "No."

Gerard set the photograph down on the table, and noticed how the other man followed it with his eyes.

"Look," Sykes said, his tone growing testy, "do you mind if I talk to the cops to see if anything's missing?"

Gerard gestured graciously. "By all means."

When Sykes headed back for the bedroom, Gerard repocketed the photograph and headed out the front door.

As he crossed the quiet street, Biggs and Renfro caught up to him.

"He's pulling our chain, Sam," Renfro said. The air was cold, and his words formed a trail of white mist as he fell in step beside his boss. "If this was the guy Kimble was looking for, why call us?"

Gerard said nothing for a few seconds. Biggs was watching him keenly; his expression was one of curiosity mixed with growing doubt, the same look he had worn since that morning, when Kimble had fled the federal lockup. When Gerard had failed to do his job.

The winter sun behind the three men cast crisp shadows on the asphalt in front of their feet. Gerard looked down at his own—as elusive as Kimble, always just a half step beyond his reach.

"Kimble said he's putting together a puzzle. We don't need to put it together, too—we just need to be there when he gets to the next piece."

He stopped, and looked over his shoulder at Sykes's apartment, then back at his two deputies. "Keep somebody on him. If he moves, I want to know."

After he left Sykes's apartment, Kimble got on the el and rode for a while, staring out at the cityscape.

Sykes. Lentz. Devlin-Macgregor. RDU90. They were all connected to each other; all connected to Helen's death.

All connected to those damned biopsy reports from Lentz that had shown perfectly normal results, when they should have shown diseased liver tissue.

Something about a biopsy report I returned to you? Lentz had asked that night. The night of January 20 . . .

Yeah, Kimble heard himself say in his memory. *Three.*

But there had been another liver after that, hadn't there? He'd assumed it had been a paperwork screwup at first, but there had been another RDU90 patient with a bad liver that very night—the bleeder he'd assisted Tom Price with.

They had hauled him off to jail, and he had never seen *that* biopsy report—but he had a hunch it had come back exactly the same way as all the others. Normal. And how many other RDU90 patients had suffered the same liver damage over the past several months? How many of them had died?

Lentz was intentionally falsifying the reports. But why?

Kimble got off at the stop for Chicago Memorial Hospital, and headed over familiar turf for the medical library. It took him less than thirty minutes to do a subject search on the library computer and find what he sought: an article in a medical investing periodical entitled, "Devlin-Macgregor Expects Pay Dirt with Provasic: Pharmaceutical company plans to go public on introduction of new drug, Provasic (RDU90)."

Kimble looked up from the article, convinced now that Helen's murder had not been the result of a botched burglary. Someone had wanted to kill *him*, Kimble, and Helen had gotten in the way. He found a Devlin-Macgregor prospectus and slipped it into his jacket.

He went outside and found a secluded pay phone, and dialed a number he was amazed to find he still remembered. He could barely make out the worn number stamped above the pay phone's dial pad; he left it with the answering service, hung up, and waited.

In less than a minute, the telephone rang. He picked it up at once and said, "Can you talk?"

"Richard?" Charlie Nichols said. Kimble closed his free ear with a finger. The connection was poor, and in the background there was a hubbub of voices; it sounded as if Nichols were in a crowded meeting. "Yes," Nichols said, in a voice almost too low to hear. "I'm on a hotel phone. What's going on?"

Kimble spoke rapid-fire. "I found him, Charlie. I found the guy that killed Helen."

"What . . . ?" Nichols whispered, then fell speechless.

"It's all about a drug, Charlie. They tried to kill *me* because of a drug."

"Who?"

"Devlin-Macgregor and Lentz. Lentz was supervising the RDU90 protocol. He knew I'd found out the drug had problems. It's Lentz."

Nichols was silent again, this time for so long that Kimble felt a stab of fear—maybe Nichols didn't believe him, thought the charges were crazy. Maybe Nichols had made friends with Lentz over the past months and couldn't accept the idea of his guilt.

Kimble was on the verge of hanging up out of panic when Nichols finally spoke, in a tone dulled by shock and reluctance.

"Richard . . . Lentz is dead. He died in an auto accident last summer."

Kimble leaned his forehead against the cold metal of the pay phone and surrendered to the downward-spiraling pull of despair. Lentz could not be dead.

Could *not* be. How else could he incriminate Sykes, tie him in to Helen's death . . . ?

And then he raised his head as he saw himself standing over Tim Price's bleeder and saying to the nurse . . . *make sure you get Kath a slice . . .*

"Can you prove this about the drug?" Nichols was asking.

"I need your help," Kimble said firmly. "Call Mr. Roosevelt and tell him I'm coming in."

In the conference room at the U.S. Marshal's Office, the group Gerard had come to think of as the Fearless Foursome—Biggs, Poole, Renfro, and Newman—sat assembled around the situation board. Gerard stood in front of it, arms folded, one hand to his chin, like a teacher contemplating a challenging math problem he has just presented to the class.

Gerard's sense of frustration had been honed to razor keenness by the repeated close encounters with Kimble—at Cook County, where he had eluded them by no more than half a day, at Sykes's apartment, where the distance had closed to less than an hour. The worst was the encounter at the lockup, where Kimble had been in their grasp, only to wriggle free because of Gerard's failure to stop him.

He was at a loss to explain why Kimble had purposely drawn them to Sykes's apartment. The others were at a loss as well, and the five of them had returned to the situation room to brainstorm.

The instant everyone had settled into place, Renfro put the question before Gerard had a chance: "If you were Richard Kimble . . . Why would you hunt for a one-armed man you think killed your wife, find him, then leave him and call us?''

From the slight scowls on the others' faces, it was clear that the question was foremost in their minds. The silence before anyone attempted to answer was oppressive.

Poole spoke first, but her tone lacked conviction. ''To throw us off his trail.''

Newman groaned softly and clicked his tongue to indicate disbelief. She turned to him, defensive. ''No, think about it. The whole thing is a ruse to divert our attention away from something else Kimble's plotting. He wants us to get so wrapped up in Sykes that we miss something . . .''

''Unless . . .'' Gerard said, stroking his chin and staring at the cards tacked on the board: Sykes. Kimble. ''What if you were a well-respected surgeon and wanted to kill your wife? How would you do it?''

Biggs still had the shadow of doubt in his eyes that Gerard had seen earlier, at the lockup, when he had seemed disturbed at the thought of killing Kimble. But he seemed in control of it, and had been working long enough with Gerard to understand that such doubt could be deadly. ''I'd hire a pro,'' Biggs said. ''Sight unseen.''

Gerard did not smile, but one corner of his mouth quirked upward with satisfaction.

Poole nodded with approval at Biggs's suggestion. ''Set it up to look like a robbery gone bad.''

Renfro leaned forward in his chair suddenly, elbows on his knees. "How would you find him? Look in the phone book?"

"Through a connection," Gerard offered, then fell silent and stood back to let his deputies figure it out. He could sense a sudden surge of enthusiasm for the line of reasoning. This was good; they would need it to overcome any doubts about Kimble's guilt. They would need it in order to capture him.

"Maybe through a company you did some business with," Poole said quickly.

Biggs was nodding. "Like a pharmaceutical company. Someone in security . . ."

Newman's pale complexion was faintly flushed as he added eagerly, "On the night of his wife's murder, Kimble attended a hospital benefit for Children's Research sponsored by Devlin-Macgregor Pharmaceutical—Sykes's company."

Gerard favored him with an approving look as he tacked a Devlin-Macgregor card onto the situation board; Newman straightened in his chair as though proud to finally have the boss's encouragement.

A faint crease appeared between Biggs's thick eyebrows. "But Sykes claims he was out of town . . ."

Poole swiveled in her chair toward him as she picked up the thread. "And company records support that he was on a business trip—"

"That's an easy fix," Renfro interrupted, waving a hand as if to erase their doubt. "So let's say he was *in* town. Did the job. Everything goes as planned—with one problem."

Newman was nodding vigorously, so obviously pleased to finally be accepted as an equal in the discussion that Gerard had to repress a smile of amusement. "Instead of looking like a robbery gone bad, Kimble ends up being the one accused—"

"—tried, convicted—" Biggs added.

Poole finished the thought and leaned back in her chair, satisfied. "—and the hit man gets away clean."

"So Kimble returns to hunt for and find the hit man," Renfro said.

Newman began to speak, then hesitated, his enthusiasm suddenly dimmed. "Why? To share the blame? He'd still go to prison. It just doesn't make sense. If he wanted to get even with Sykes, he would have waited for him and killed him."

Silence.

Newman's tone rose slightly as it turned defensive. "I mean, hasn't anyone else here considered that he might be innocent? It *is* the one explanation that makes sense."

More silence followed, and then Poole said coldly, "He was tried and convicted—"

"You're not a judge," Renfro said, before Poole had finished. "Have you read the transcript? Looked at the evidence?"

Biggs, Gerard noted, remained very silent as he watched the exchange, his expression one of uncertainty.

"No," Newman answered heatedly. "But maybe I should. Maybe we all should—"

Gerard stopped them. "We're not here to retry the case, people." He narrowed his eyes at Newman. "Let me remind you that it is not our job to contemplate Dr. Kimble's innocence or guilt. It's our job to bring him in. Got that?''

He caught himself in time before he said, *It's not our problem . . .*

Newman's mouth and eyes tensed, grew very small; his expression said he did not get it at all, but he replied, softly, "Yes, sir."

"Now," Gerard said pleasantly, "to go back to the subject: Why does Kimble hunt down the hit man? Is he trying to share the blame, as Newman says? Would he really still go to prison?" He turned to face Newman, who eyed him with a wooden expression. "You're underestimating the power of the good doctor. It would be his word against . . . Sykes's. Who would you believe?"

Newman sighed and relaxed slightly, as if allowing the point.

"So what does Kimble do next?" Biggs asked.

"Get help," Renfro suggested.

Gerard tacked another card on the board and shot Renfro a look. The card read: "NICHOLS."

Renfro gave a nod, which rippled out until all four, including Newman, were nodding in agreement.

"Newman," Gerard said, "check phone records for Sykes and Kimble." As he moved toward the door, he handed the photograph of Sykes, the fish, and the man to Biggs and said, "Find out who this guy is."

Gerard hurried out the door. As he did, Biggs promptly thrust the photograph at Newman.

Newman stared down at it sourly, then back up at Biggs, who wore a look of self-satisfaction at having rid himself of a time-consuming, unpleasant task. "Why do I get all the great jobs?"

The phone in Frederick Sykes's living room rang once. Sykes did not react, did not move toward the phone. He simply waited, and when the phone rang again—once—thirty seconds later, he drew back the curtain and peered out at the plainclothes cops sitting in the car parked down the street.

Sykes did not wonder whether he was being paranoid, whether the people were really cops or not; he had pulled enough plainclothes duty himself during his stint as a police officer to know an unmarked car and a stakeout when he saw them. He'd been a cop six years. That was when he first killed someone—a kid, pockets full of cigarettes stolen from a 7-Eleven. A kid who kept on running even after Sykes bellowed for him to stop.

Sykes shot him in the back, and discovered that he had a talent for it, and even after he left the force, he made good use of that talent. After all, killing was killing, no matter which side of the law you stood on; the only difference was who made the rules.

Sykes had never botched a job, had never even gotten nervous—except maybe with Lentz, but that was tough because they had palled around beforehand. Even so, he had done the job quickly, efficiently.

In fact, he had never had any trouble with a job until the Kimble case, which had been a screwup from the very beginning. First, Kimble hadn't been there; and then Kimble had showed at the last minute and caught Sykes entirely off guard. He had panicked for the first time in his career, and Kimble had been one impossible son of a bitch to take down. He had almost caused Sykes to get caught—and that frightened Sykes. He wanted nothing more to do with Richard Kimble, ever.

But things had worked out. Kimble had taken the rap for the wife's murder, and Sykes had gotten a paid vacation to the Caribbean, and returned a few weeks later to find everything back to normal.

Now, almost a year later, Kimble was back, and Sykes was panicking again. He no longer felt safe in his own apartment—and it was clear Kimble wouldn't stop until the cops came and hauled Sykes away.

He wanted out. He wanted to go far, far away. But there were the freaking cops hanging out in front of his apartment. And now he needed to get to a pay phone, but they'd tail him there, too. He needed to think, and fast . . .

Sykes let the curtain drop and picked up his tumbler of gin over ice from the end table, lifting it to his lips with an unsteady hand. The liquor sloshed over the edge of the glass and spilled down the front of Sykes's shirt, perfuming the air with the fragrance of juniper. He swore, then took a good hit off it before setting it down to pick up the phone with his good hand and cradle the receiver against his shoulder.

He dialed 911. A voice answered on the second ring.

"Emergency operator."

Still cradling the phone between ear and shoulder, Sykes went over to the coffee table to pick up the automatic lying there. With his left hand, he placed the gun in his right, then attached the silencer. "I want to report a fire," he said calmly. "No, it's not my place, it's a couple doors down. Number three two three Wabash Avenue. Yes, that's right . . . Thank you."

He tucked the gun into his waistband, hung up the phone, took another hit from the tumbler, then moved over to the window to watch.

Within five minutes, he heard the wail of the sirens. Seconds later, a pair of fire trucks turned onto the street and pulled up, parking across the street from the unmarked car—blocking it completely from view.

Sykes smiled, retrieved his jacket and slipped into it. The street was a war zone when he walked out into it, filled with people swarming out of the building, firemen, patrol cars. The two large fire engines entirely blocked the front of the building from the view of those on the other side of the street. Sykes whistled as he strolled out and walked calmly away, unseen, to make the phone call that would determine Richard Kimble's fate.

11

By the time Kimble arrived at Chicago Memorial Hospital, the morning sun had disappeared beneath pewter clouds heavy with snow. He entered unseen through the loading dock and took the back stairs down to the morgue in the basement. Before he dared enter, he knocked tentatively, three times, on the closed door.

The heavy door swung slowly open. Behind it stood Roosevelt, stooped, silver-haired, smiling. Roosevelt was ancient and apparently immortal; he had been working at C.M.H. at least two decades longer than any other fellow employee's memory extended, and was such an institution that no one was quite sure whether Roosevelt was his last name or his first. The staff referred to him simply as Old Mr. Roosevelt.

"Sure is good to see you again, Dr. Kimble," the old man said softly, in a wavering, reedy voice. His smile widened, showing yellowed, coffee-stained teeth.

"You, too, Roosevelt. Been a long time." Kimble returned the smile, as overwhelmed by gratitude as he had been the day Charlie Nichols had said, *Anything . . . I'll get you more money. Some clothes . . . Here, take my coat . . .*

Roosevelt had not aged an iota in the year Kimble had been gone, looked the same as he had since the first day Kimble had come to work at Chicago Memorial. But he knew that Roosevelt was staring up now into the face of a much, much older man.

Roosevelt grasped the edge of the door with one strong, bony hand and gestured with the other for Kimble to enter swiftly. Kimble hurried inside as the old man peered through wire-rimmed spectacles down the hallway to be sure no one watched, then closed the door. The sound echoed in the brightly lit, silent morgue.

Roosevelt put a hand on Kimble's elbow and drew him past gurneys on which draped, still forms lay, past shining stainless-steel autopsy tables waiting to be put to use, into a second room where tissue samples were stored inside a temperature-controlled vault.

"Roosevelt," Kimble said as they walked, "I can't thank you enough . . ."

The research assistant raised a palm, then let it drop, indicating that the very thought was ridiculous. "I'm not doing this for you, Dr. Kimble, I'm doing it for me." He glanced sidewise at Kimble and showed him another slice of yellowed teeth. "You were always the best of all the surgeons to work with, believe me. Some of them can get pretty high and mighty, but you—you were always nice. Hasn't been the same around here since you left."

Kimble waited while the old man disappeared into the storage area. Seconds later, Roosevelt returned, with an expanding manila folder and a small plastic slide box. "This is the RDU90 file and the samples Dr. Nichols said you needed. I set 'em aside for you right after he called."

Kimble took them eagerly. "Thanks, Roosevelt." He looked up at the old man and felt a wave of guilt. He was already worried about involving Charles, who now faced the threat of jail if caught aiding a fugitive; he couldn't bear the thought of causing old Roosevelt any trouble. "Look, I want you to promise me something . . ."

"Anything for you, Dr. Kimble."

"If anyone sees me . . . If anything happens . . . You mustn't tell them that Dr. Nichols called you."

"Well, of course not." Roosevelt straightened his glasses with thumb and forefinger and gazed up at Kimble with mild indignation, his eyes magnified behind bifocal lenses. "It goes without saying. And I'll never tell 'em I saw you, don't worry. If I can put up with tired, cranky interns and residents, I most surely can deal with the police . . ."

"That's not what I mean. If anything goes wrong and they figure out I've been here, you have to tell them that I forced you to hand over the samples. At gunpoint, understand?''

Roosevelt pursed his lips and frowned.

"Promise me." Kimble forced his tone to lighten. "Otherwise—how can you help me again if they haul you off to jail? It's a crime to help a fugitive."

"I know," the old man said stiffly. "But you're no fugitive. You're the most pleasant vascular surgeon I ever had to deal with."

"Promise me . . ."

"Oh, all right, Dr. Kimble. I reckon we don't want to get Dr. Nichols in trouble, after all, even if he isn't near as nice to deal with."

Kimble released a short laugh. "Thanks again, Roosevelt." He turned and began moving swiftly for the exit.

"Good luck," Roosevelt called softly after him.

Kimble half turned without stopping. "Don't forget your promise."

"Oh, I won't," Roosevelt said, and waited until he heard Kimble's footsteps recede and the door to the morgue close before he added: "In a pig's eye."

Sykes caught a cab to the el station. At a deserted pay phone kiosk, he dialed a number from memory, left a phony name and the pay phone number with the answering service, then hung up and waited.

Within two minutes, the pay phone rang. Sykes picked it up, and before he could speak, the voice on the other end of the line gave him the instructions he needed. He hung up the phone looking forward to another all-expense-paid vacation when his work was done.

Kimble hurried down the corridor toward the small research lab. Everything was going according to plan, but he still could not overcome his guilt at letting others—Charles, Roosevelt, and now Kathy—become involved.

If anything happened to any of them . . .

As he opened the glass double doors that led back to Kath Wahlund's tiny lab, he repressed the thought. Nothing would happen to them because he simply would not allow it; he simply could not bear for such a reality to come into existence. For the first time, he felt himself slowly emerging from the hell of the past year; for the first time, he considered that his life might have some meaning beyond that of bringing Frederick Sykes to justice.

He opened the door to the lab and slipped in quietly, then pulled the door to behind him.

Wahlund was absorbed in her work and did not hear. She sat huddled at the electron microscope with her back to him. At the sight of her worn, scarred leather jacket, Kimble grinned with affection. And then she turned a profile toward him as she reached for a slide from the stack beside her, and he saw that, instead of her traditional T-shirt, she wore a silky, multicolored blouse.

He stole up beside Wahlund, who kept her eyes to the microscope as she reached, without looking, for another slide from the stack.

Kimble got his hand on it first and held it firmly in place.

Wahlund tugged at it, scowled, then turned to see what was holding it. At the sight of Kimble, her mouth dropped open, and she sprang to her feet.

"Oh, my God! Richard!"

She threw her arms around him and squeezed until he could not draw a breath; he squeezed back, feeling the sting of blinked-back tears, the unquestioning and enthusiastic welcome reducing him to temporary speechlessness. And then he held her back at arm's length and they grinned at each other, Wahlund unashamedly wiping the corners of her eyes with a knuckle.

"Hey, Kath . . ." he said softly. "I loaned you some things a year ago. I need them back . . ."

In his tiny cubicle of an office, Newman sat and stared at the photograph of Frederick Sykes, the fish, and the unknown man, and prayed for inspiration. After his humiliating capture by Copeland, he wanted to be something other than a burden to the U.S. Marshal's Office; he wanted to prove his usefulness. He wanted, if such a thing was possible, to save the day.

But at the moment, inspiration proved elusive. Newman stared dully at the two men in the picture. It seemed clear that they must have been on a company junket together; the unknown man was younger, much better dressed than Sykes, clearly wealthier, not the type to rub shoulders with an ex-cop. Sykes's apartment indicated he was hardly well-to-do, not the type to be able to afford much in the way of vacations, though it was possible he was one of those eccentrics who kept thousands in cash in shopping bags around the house.

Still, Newman doubted it. Instinct told him that this was an outing sponsored by Devlin-Macgregor; both men wore lightweight parkas sporting the company logo. He could always take the photo to Devlin-Macgregor and start asking questions, but instinct also told him that this was a lousy idea. If others at the company were involved with Sykes, they would be unlikely to give accurate information; and Newman did not want to tip them off.

He wanted to figure things out for himself. Besides, his intuition insisted that there was something *there,* in the photograph, that held the key to the man's identity; something he had seen with his subconscious but not yet registered with his waking mind.

He opened his top desk drawer, removed a magnifying glass, and held it over the picture of the young well-dressed man. Not much to see, really, except that the man wore no rings, nor did he have the impression on his finger left by a wedding band recently removed. His jogging shoes were name-brand hundred-dollar models, top of the line; his watch was a Rolex.

Newman hunched forward and brought his face closer to the glass, straining to find that one clue that would salvage his battered dignity.

Next to the unfastened zipper of the man's

parka—wide open, with the sleeves pushed up because apparently the day had grown warm—was a different logo on the left breast of his polo shirt: the initials "C.M.H."

Newman set the glass atop the photo and raised his face to stare wonderingly at the blank wall opposite his desk.

C.M.H. C.M.H. He had seen these initials before recently, in the context of Richard Kimble. The "C" obviously had to stand for "Chicago," and the "M . . ."

"Medical?" Newman asked himself aloud. "Chicago Medical—"

And then a flash. "H" stood for "Hospital." Chicago Memorial, not Medical, Hospital, the place where Richard Kimble practiced medicine for so many years.

Newman rose, snatched the photograph out from under the glass, and hurried out into the hall. "Inspector Gerard—!"

As he passed the other deputies' offices, Biggs called out to him. "Sam's gone to pay a little visit to Nichols."

Newman turned, peered into the office to see Biggs sitting with his feet up on his desk, frowning at his own situation board. He waved the photograph at the deputy. "I know where he works—!"

Biggs's eyes widened; he took his feet off the desk and rose. "Well, hell . . . Let's go."

* * *

Gerard watched Charles Nichols leave the hotel conference room and head down the hallway—then recoil when he caught sight of Gerard and Renfro waiting for him. Nichols recovered admirably; there was only a split second of hesitation when Nichols looked as if he might bolt and run the other way, only a split second when Gerard saw a look of terror cross his face.

And then Nichols collected himself, so quickly that Renfro did not appear to notice. The doctor approached the two men with a gracious nod.

"Mr. Gerard."

"Doctor," Gerard said, by way of greeting. "Could I have a minute?" He gestured with his chin at a nearby empty conference room.

Nichols nodded. The three men entered; Renfro closed the door behind him. Nichols faced Gerard with a smooth, impassive expression—too smooth, Gerard decided.

He waited for Renfro to return and hand Nichols a photocopy of the picture of Sykes, the man, and the fish. Nichols stared at it without reaction.

"The man on the left is Frederick Sykes," Renfro explained, craning his neck to see over Nichols's shoulder. "He's a security specialist at Devlin-Macgregor Pharmaceuticals. Kimble broke into his apartment."

Nichols shook his head. "I don't know him." He handed the picture back to Renfro while fastening his gaze on Gerard. "You're getting pretty desperate, aren't you, Mr. Gerard? I told you, you wouldn't find Richard."

Gerard held him with The Look for a time and said nothing. There was something wrong here, something he could not put his finger on. He had no doubt that Nichols was lying, but the lie was too cold, too polished to be that of a friend covering for a friend. The deception ran deeper than that.

"Dr. Kimble hasn't come back to you for help, has he?" Gerard asked.

Nichols didn't blink, didn't look away, didn't back down from Gerard's stony gaze. "No. And it seems like we've been over this ground before. Now, if you'll excuse me . . ." He moved for the door.

"Dr. Nichols," Gerard called softly, and Nichols stopped with his back to him. "Do you know the other man in the photograph?" He held the picture out.

Nichols turned slowly, glanced at the photograph in Gerard's hand, and shook his head. "I never saw him before."

He left, closing the door behind him. Gerard stood staring at the door for some time.

In a secluded corner of Kath Wahlund's lab, Kimble huddled over a drawer flipping through file names of samples. His luck was holding: Kath had informed him that only samples over two years old were removed and archived.

Even so, Kimble felt a ripple of panic as he grew closer to the end of his search. What if Lentz or Sykes had learned of the extra slices Kimble had sent to Wahlund's lab as a precaution, and destroyed them?

No. Impossible. No one involved with the Provasic study or Devlin-Macgregor knew he'd sent the extra samples to Wahlund's lab, and no one had any reason to suspect because it wasn't standard procedure. Even Kath herself had been too swamped with work to register the oddity of it and ask him about it. But when the first biopsy report from Lentz came back screwy, Kimble had started diverting extra slices to Wahlund, as a precaution against what he saw as sloppy lab work.

Ultimately, he would have gone to Kath and had her check his samples against Lentz's—but his life had been shattered before he could do so.

As he rifled through the sample names, Kimble suddenly had the curious sense of being outside time, an observer looking back to a year ago and seeing the moment when his fate had forked off in two directions.

Helen should not have died. He should have come here a year ago, found the samples, blown the whistle on Lentz and Devlin-Macgregor. He and Helen should have been happy.

Instead, he was an escaped fugitive, standing here beside Kath Wahlund, searching desperately for the evidence that could clear his name. Somehow, he had been forced onto a path, a fate, which did not belong to him, a path he should never have been forced to travel.

Kimble came to himself and realized that he was staring at a group of slides marked *R. KIMBLE*.

He grabbed them and hurried over to Kath, who sat working at her microscope. Wahlund set aside the slide she was looking at—one of Lentz's, from the Provasic study—and took Kimble's samples.

"Okay . . ." Kath murmured, intent. "Let's take a look." She leaned over the eyepiece as Kimble loaded the first sample for her. "Hmmmm . . ."

Kimble hovered over her. "Half the people in the study were indigents. No follow-up, no baseline on them. Who could say they didn't come into the study with bad livers?"

As he spoke, Kath removed the slide and took another one, then repeated the process three more times without comment—but the furrows in her forehead deepened until she was openly scowling.

She turned to Kimble and moved aside, motioning for him to take a look for himself. "The one on the right is one of the samples you sent me. It shows a lot of inflammation loaded with eosinophils. When you see that with the accumulation of bile, it's a classic for—"

Kimble interrupted, rising. "—drug-induced hepatitis."

She nodded. "I'm impressed. Now, look at this . . ." She lifted the slide from Lentz's box of samples and positioned it, glancing at it to be sure it was correctly focused, then leaned aside so Kimble could take a look. "According to the study, this is a slice from the same liver."

Kimble peered through the eyepiece. The difference between the two samples of tissue was marked. "Cold normal," he said, straightening.

"Clearly *not* from the same tissue," Kath said. "Those dirty sons of bitches . . ."

Kimble rubbed a hand over his face, suddenly feeling a surge of hopelessness and the exhaustion of too many near-sleepless nights. "But how can we prove their slides were the ones switched? They can simply say that I faked my slides in an effort to clear myself—"

Kath's smile was tight, small, coldly triumphant. "In fact," she said, yielding the microscope again to Kimble, "see this small area of bile duct proliferation? Von Meyenberg's Complex. Occurs in only two percent of the population. But it's in every one of Lentz's five samples."

Kimble looked up, too tired to instantly make the connection. "That's statistically impossible."

Her smile widened to a full grin. "That's because they're all from the same liver." She reached up to put a hand on his shoulder. "That offer to testify on your behalf still stands, you know. You've got them, Richard. You've got them . . ."

Kimble sagged weakly against the wall, at that moment feeling as if the two threads of his unraveled fate had suddenly rewoven themselves together, more tightly than ever, and he was once again standing where and when and with whom he belonged.

At that same moment, Newman and Biggs had just seated themselves in the office of the Chicago Memorial Hospital Personnel Director, Betty Mikopoulos. Mikopoulos was a slender, quick-moving person, brimming with a restless energy that made Newman nervous. She stared down through oversized tortoise-shell glasses at the picture of the young man with the "C.M.H." emblazoned on his polo shirt and looked up at the two deputies with a nod.

"Yes, he was a doctor here."

Newman brightened, for a split second permitting himself to indulge in a daydream of himself on a platform, being given a commendation and promotion for cracking the investigation wide open and proving Kimble's innocence, much to Gerard's disgruntlement and Kimble's eternal gratitude. Both men were sitting in the audience, applauding. "You recognize him?" Newman said hopefully, extricating himself from the daydream. "Do you have an address for him in your personnel files?"

She handed the photo back to him. "His name's Lentz. A pathologist. I didn't know him personally, and I don't think an address will do you much good. I only remember him because he died last summer."

Newman wilted as he and Biggs exchanged a look; Newman's daydream evaporated with a small mental *pop*. Dead witnesses were not very helpful to an investigation.

But Newman persisted. "Anybody down in pathology who might know something about the guy?"

Mikopoulos hesitated, and glanced at the clock behind them on the wall; Newman turned, and saw that it was two minutes past six o'clock. Outside, the sky was already darkening.

"It's kinda late to catch anyone," Mikopoulos said. "But you might go by the morgue. Just take the elevators down to the basement and follow the signs. There's an old guy down there, a Mr. Roosevelt, who's been around forever. He knows everything about everybody.''

''Thank you,'' Newman said politely. He and Biggs left and headed for the elevator.

Biggs's mood had soured the instant Mikopoulos said that Lentz was dead; Newman kept wanting to say something encouraging, but he could think of nothing. Neither spoke on the ride down to the basement—not until they got off the elevators and had followed the signs through the dimly lit corridors to the morgue.

At the doorway, Biggs hesitated, his lip curling. ''Just what I want to do before dinner.''

''Come on,'' Newman said with faint impatience, feeling his hope of ever being accepted by the marshals dwindling. He pushed open the heavy door, and forced himself not to react to the sight inside: A stooped old man was moving a woman's naked corpse from a gurney onto a stainless steel autopsy table pushed alongside. He looked up, startled, the heels of the dead woman's feet in his hands as Biggs and Newman entered.

''Can I help you?'' The old man angled the woman's legs onto the steel table, then caught her under the arms and swung the torso over, completing the move.

Newman tried not to look at the dead woman, tried not to notice the other draped bodies surrounding them as he replied, ''Are you Mr. Roosevelt?''

''Yes.'' Roosevelt covered the woman discreetly

213

with a sheet, as if embarrassed for her, then stared back at Newman and Biggs with yellowing, watery eyes made huge by the thick lenses of his metal-framed glasses.

Biggs produced his I.D. "We're United States marshals. We're trying to find out some information about a pathologist named Lentz. He used to be on staff here."

The old man's eyes suddenly went small; a chill descended over his expression. "He's dead."

Newman took a step closer and tried, without success, to emulate the polite yet utterly intimidating look of which Gerard was master. "Yeah, we heard. We wanted to know if he knew or had any contact with a Dr. Richard Kimble."

Roosevelt took a step back, looked quickly from Newman to Biggs. His lips parted, and Newman thought he saw a tremor in them. "I . . ." The old man faltered. "I haven't seen Dr. Kimble."

Biggs shot Newman a look that was pure electricity; both men instinctively took another step closer to Roosevelt.

"That's not what I asked, sir," Newman said softly, his heartbeat quickening. "I just wanted to know if Dr. Kimble and Dr. Lentz knew each other."

"I . . . I don't know." There was a tremor now, no mistake, and it was in Roosevelt's voice. "Excuse me, I got to go." He turned as if to run.

Biggs took two giant steps and was in front of the old man in a flash. "I think you're lying to us."

The old man turned, his expression stricken,

toward Newman, who was entirely unable to repress a faint, self-satisfied smile.

Kimble sat in Kath's lab reading Lentz's report while Kath carefully repacked both sets of slides for him. He looked up from the folder and shook his head, overwhelmed by the sorrowful anger.

"They'd be home free if I hadn't been leaning on them to account for the livers I was seeing. And I wouldn't have seen the livers if I hadn't told the guys on my service to call me when they had cases that were bleeding excessively in surgery."

He did not allow himself to say, *And if I hadn't told the guys on my service to call me, Helen would still be alive . . .*

"Big bucks," Kath said, her tone bitter, sarcastic. "One schmuck standing in the way. Easy, get rid of him and his wife." She paused. "But why Lentz? He just didn't seem the type . . ."

"Why not?" Kimble slipped out the Devlin-Macgregor prospectus he had taken from the medical library and waved it at her. "He's one of the original patent holders. Toss the samples I sent, replace them with healthy samples, issue the path report on the healthy stuff . . . piece of cake."

He sighed as she snapped the lid shut on the box of slides and went back to looking at Lentz's report, leafing through to the end. Amazingly, all of the reports had been signed . . . by Lentz himself. He glanced up as Kathy rose and walked over to him with the box.

"Kath . . . when did Lentz die?"

She shrugged as she handed him the box. "Oh, last summer sometime. August. Why?"

"Because a good third of the samples Lentz approved were signed after he died." He held open the folder so she could see; Lentz's signature was on reports dated October, November, December. "Someone else used Lentz's name." Even as he said it, he felt a growing sense of unease, of a revelation so horrible that his conscious mind suppressed it.

With a feeling of ominousness, he flipped open the Devlin-Macgregor prospectus to the first page.

And saw there a photograph of one of the recently appointed members of the board of directors, Dr. Charles Nichols.

Kimble rose, numbed and blinded by an invisible blizzard. He stuffed the prospectus into his bag along with the samples and Lentz's report.

Kath saw the change in his expression and glanced up, concerned. "Where are you going?"

Somehow his lips moved; somehow he spoke.

"To see an old friend," he told Kath, and left her to stare after him.

12

The lights were on in the U.S. Marshal's Office. Seated at his desk, Gerard looked up to find Poole in the doorway. "It's Newman. Line two."

Newman's voice conveyed such brisk confidence, such self-satisfaction, that at first Gerard did not recognize it. "Newman here. You'll remember we called you at the Hilton to let you know we were going to check out the Sykes photo at C.M.H. . . ."

"Yes?" Gerard put it on the speaker so Renfro could hear.

"Kimble apparently just left here a few hours ago. We've got a positive I.D. on the photo—the man posing with Sykes is Dr. Alexander Lentz, a pathologist at C.M.H. He died last August, but up to then he was doing a study on a drug called RDU90 for a company called Devlin-Macgregor." Newman paused dramatically to let the words sink in. "Right now Biggs is questioning a Mr. Roosevelt who works here at C.M.H. Roosevelt just saw Kimble no more than an hour ago."

"Where's he headed?" Gerard demanded.

"The old guy didn't know where he was going. But he picked up some tissue samples."

"Tissue samples?"

"From a drug study. And signed for by Dr. Charles Nichols."

Gerard and Renfro exchanged a look.

"Nichols also knew Lentz," Newman continued.

"He was covering for Kimble," Renfro said swiftly.

Gerard was not surprised—that much had been apparent. He recalled Nichols's too-perfect tan, too-perfect hair and teeth, too-perfect composure when his gaze had flickered over the photo of Sykes and Lentz.

I never saw him before . . .

Nichols's brittle surface was so gleaming, so blindingly reflective that Gerard couldn't get a read. He felt once again that he was missing something, something that had to do with the cool insolence in Nichols's eyes—the look Gerard had expected to find in Kimble's booking photo, and had not.

"Good work, Newman," he said brusquely. Beside him, Renfro rolled his eyes; but in the silence on the other end of the line, Gerard could practically hear Newman beam. "Now where are those phone records for Sykes and Kimble I asked you to get?"

"Uh, well, sir, I'll have those for you as soon as—"

Gerard hung up.

Kimble made his way through the underground network of steam tunnels, known only to veteran C.M.H. staff, and emerged aboveground only a short distance away from the el station.

Outside, the sun had already set. Even so, the sky had not darkened to black, but remained an opaque slate color because of the thick layer of clouds. The snow was not yet visible, but an occasional flake, cold and wet, kissed his face as he strode across the hospital grounds toward the station.

The sight of Charles Nichols's picture in the Devlin-Macgregor prospectus had evoked shock and anger and grief that translated itself into an aching physical heaviness that settled over Kimble's heart.

He had been wrong, so wrong about Charlie. So very wrong . . .

Kimble raised a hand to his face as he stepped into the busy station, tried to collect himself as he rubbed shoulders with fast-moving strangers. There was no point in blaming himself; it would probably have made no difference whether Nichols had been a close friend or a mere acquaintance. The end result would have been the same.

But why was Charlie pretending to be so helpful now—offering money, help, arranging for Kimble to pick up the very samples that would incriminate Devlin-Macgregor?

The only logical answer caused Kimble to glance over his shoulder, pick up his pace. The downtown el was just pulling away as he neared; he broke into a run at the last minute, and managed to leap onto the front car.

The car was uncrowded. Kimble sat down across from a man reading a newspaper and tried to think.

He needed protection; he needed to go to the police. But he simply didn't have enough evidence—yet—to tie Sykes to Helen's murder. All he had were some slides that showed that test results on a drug were faked, not enough to clear himself of murder charges. The cops would ignore him.

Not my problem . . .

Even Walter Gutherie, his own lawyer, didn't believe in his innocence. Once he went to prison, he could forget about convincing anyone to investigate Sykes, Nichols, Devlin-Macgregor.

What he needed was something to tie Sykes and Nichols together. And failing that—

Failing that, he would just as soon die running.

Either way, he had to see Charlie Nichols, had to hear the truth from Charlie's own lips. Had to have the satisfaction of confronting him. There was nothing left to lose.

And if he could get a confession . . .

Kimble had been idly gazing, unfocused, at the front page of the newspaper across from him for some time before his conscious mind finally registered what was written there, in a small headline near the bottom of the page:

KIMBLE IN CHICAGO

Above the headline, his booking photo stared back at him.

Kimble looked away, thinking to get up and move, as the man turned the pages. But where could he flee? How many other newspapers were there on the train, and how could he know who had read them, and would remember the booking photo?

He froze, panicking, as the man glanced over the newspaper at him, then folded it back to the front page.

It would be all right, Kimble told himself; so long as he kept his head down, so long as he didn't move quickly, the man would never suspect anything. He'd had a beard in the booking photo, and—

The man peered over the paper at Kimble again, then swiftly looked back down.

And rose, folding the paper and tucking it under his arm with exaggerated casualness. Kimble raised his hand to his face and turned away as the man hurried into one of the rear cars.

To find a cop, no doubt. Kimble looked out the window. His stop was coming up next, in only a minute or two. If he could just hold on till then . . .

He got up and moved into the center aisle in order to see into the next car.

The man with the newspaper had found a transit cop, all right, and was showing him Kimble's photograph and pointing to the front car. The cop raised a radio to his lips—and then someone stepped from the rear of the car into the aisle in front of Kimble, blocking his view.

Kimble frowned, leaned to one side, trying to get

a better view . . . then realized that the man approaching him held a gun, and looked up into the grimly smiling face of Frederick Sykes.

Gerard looked up from the situation board as Newman appeared in his office doorway with a stack of papers in his hand.

"I have those phone records for you, boss." Newman's eyes were bloodshot, his tone one of exhaustion as he stepped inside, gesturing with the papers.

Gerard noticed the term of address with an inward smile—Newman had never referred to him before as anything other than "sir," and this new familiarity was no doubt due to his newfound confidence and Gerard's restrained encouragement.

At the same time, he detected a note of defeat in Newman's tone. He held the younger man's gaze until at last Newman surrendered and answered the question in his superior's eyes.

"I checked Sykes's calls for the last two years against Kimble's, like you asked," he said disconsolately. "And found nothing."

"All right." Gerard directed his attention back to the situation board. "It was a thought."

Newman did not leave. Gerard sensed his presence, turned, and lifted his dark brows quizzically.

Newman sighed, clearly disheartened by the information he was about to relay. "But when I cross-checked Kimble's phone records . . . one came up."

For a few seconds, neither spoke. And then Gerard said, in a low voice, "Kimble called Sykes." He half rose out of his chair and shouted at the corridor, so loudly that Newman jumped, "Renfro! Get C.P.D. to bring in Sykes!"

Gerard settled into his chair and leaned slowly back—away from the desk, away from Newman, away from this unwanted revelation. "When?" he asked, more out of reflex than a desire to know.

"Night of his wife's murder. Seven-thirty in the evening, from his car."

"I see," Gerard said slowly. He propped his elbows on his desk and steepled his hands, lowering his face toward them as if in an attitude of prayer. He thought of Kimble's booking photo, and the look in his eyes, and felt a sense of loss, an inability to comprehend; he thought of his own steady refusal to believe in Kimble's innocence and congratulated himself, but there was no pleasure in it.

Newman watched him, seemed to sense his doubt, and said, as if defending his words, "I have the phone record right here . . ."

Another thought seized Gerard and he turned toward the doorway, yelling, "Poole! Bring me Kimble's arrest report. Now!" He looked up, caught Newman's defensive posture, and said, "No, Newman . . . I believe you."

He expected the younger man to leave then, but Newman lingered as Poole appeared in the doorway with the transcript and handed it to Gerard. Gerard took it, set it down on his desk as Poole retreated and Renfro appeared, his narrow face taut.

"Sam—" Renfro's voice was slightly higher-pitched than normal. "C.P.D. just checked Sykes's apartment. He's not there. They've issued an A.P.B.''

"Hell," Gerard said. His first impulse was to take swift action, but there was nothing they could do until someone reported sighting Sykes. He could not fathom where Sykes was headed, but he suspected that, wherever it was, Richard Kimble would not be far away.

Renfro just as quickly disappeared, and Newman, who had watched all of this in silence, turned to go— but stopped in the doorway and turned toward Gerard, his tone one of confusion. "I just don't understand."

Gerard looked up, expectant.

"I just . . .'' Newman faltered, turned his face toward the corridor as if suddenly embarrassed. "I can't—'' He broke off and turned back suddenly to Gerard, his gaze intently curious. "Have you ever had a hunch, Inspector? A really *strong* hunch, one you were willing to stake everything on?"

Gerard nodded behind steepled hands and did not quite meet Newman's eyes. "Yes. I've had hunches before."

"Were they usually right?"

Gerard nodded, slowly.

"I just don't understand," Newman said. "I was just so sure he was innocent . . . Maybe I'm just not cut out for this kind of work after all."

Gerard said nothing as Newman turned abruptly and left.

Gerard stared after him a time. It would have been easy to surrender at that moment to the damning logic of the phone records; it would have been easy to dismiss the look in Kimble's eyes and say it had all been a mistake. After all, they had everything they needed to convince themselves of Kimble's guilt.

And yet . . .

Gerard flipped open the file containing Kimble's arrest transcript. He had no idea what he was looking for, but he knew that, whatever it was, it had damned well better be here. As Newman might say, he had a hunch.

"**B**ack up," Sykes said, and gestured with the gun. "Move to the door, Doc."

Kimble did as he was ordered, backing slowly away from Sykes and lifting his hands to show he was unarmed. The train was less than a minute away from the next stop, but he had run out of time, and Sykes blocked his only means of escape. He glanced over his shoulder toward the oncoming station.

Sykes caught his look and advanced toward him. "This is my stop, Doc."

"Good," Kimble said. He felt no fear, only perfect, one-pointed, all-consuming rage. "It's my stop, too." He took another step backwards, toward the side exit.

The door behind Sykes snapped open. A uniformed transit cop—the one whom Kimble had seen talking to the man with the newspaper—stepped onto the car.

"Kimble," the cop said softly. He was young,

slender, wide-eyed at the sight of an escaped prisoner; the gun in his hand shook slightly. He called to
Sykes, who stood with his back to him. "Sir, move
away from him."

Sykes turned and pumped four bullets into the
young man's chest; the cop fell, slammed backward
against a row of seats.

In the split second before Sykes fired, Kimble
threw himself against the exit, braced himself against
a handrail, and pulled on the emergency brake above
the door.

The floor beneath him lurched. Kimble held on as
the brakes locked with an ear-splitting screech. In the
next car, bags, briefcases, bodies went flying through
the air. Sykes was propelled backwards, toward Kimble; the gun was knocked from his grasp and skittered across the floor, coming to rest inches from the
body of the wounded cop.

Kimble dove for it. Sykes reared up, catching him
in the stomach, hurling him back against the wall, but
he recovered, bounding back to slam Sykes against a
pole. On hands and knees, he crawled, got to the gun,
a .38—

What kind of gun did he have?

*It was . . . a thirty-eight, I think. I only saw it for a
second . . .*

—and aimed it at Sykes while he took the gun
from the limp hand of the cop.

Sykes bared yellow teeth. "Go ahead. You don't
have it in you."

Kimble raised the gun with a barely perceptible
tremor, lip twitching as he took one step, then an-

other, toward Sykes, until both guns were aimed directly at Sykes's skull. His gaze was fixed on Sykes's face, but he saw only Helen's hand, sticky with blood as he gently lifted it away from her wounded head, only to uncover shattered bone and brain . . .

Sykes's lips parted as the barrels neared his head, as he stared into Kimble's face and saw the madness there; his dark eyes gleamed with fear.

Kimble's finger tightened on the trigger of Sykes's weapon. Fitting. It was only fitting, to kill him with the gun that had killed Helen . . .

He almost fired. At the last second, he seized control of himself and whipped the gun in his right hand across Sykes's face. Blood spattered from Sykes's nose, lightly spraying Kimble. He gritted his teeth, lips drawing back in a grimace of anger at Sykes and disgust at himself, and hit Sykes with the butt of the gun—despite his fury choosing those areas of the skull least likely to fracture, least likely to cause death or permanent damage, careful to avoid the temples.

Sykes whimpered and took a step back, throwing up his hands in a useless effort to shield himself. Kimble struck again.

Again. Again, driving Sykes backwards down the aisle until they had traveled the length of the car, until Sykes's knees buckled and he sank, unconscious, to the floor.

Kimble tucked Sykes's gun in his belt and moved immediately over to the young cop to check for a pulse. There was none—just as Kimble had known from the moment Sykes had fired and the four bullets had torn open the young man's chest. He pulled the handcuffs and keys from the cop's belt, dragged Sykes over by the wrist, and cuffed him to the dead man. The keys he pocketed.

And then he paused, crouching over Sykes's still form, and lifted the unconscious man's head by its dark, curling hair.

"Not as easy as Helen, was it?" Kimble whispered bitterly, then let go and let Sykes's head drop. "You missed your stop . . ."

He rose and hurried to the front of the car, both guns in his hands. The train had stopped just short of the station, with only the first two windows of the car overlooking the platform. Kimble hopped onto the seat, kicked out the window, and jumped out onto the station platform.

In his brightly lit office, Gerard nursed his twelfth cup of coffee for the day as he stared down at the transcript of Kelly and Rosetti's interrogation of Richard Kimble the night of January 20. He was beginning to yield to Newman's sense of despair, beginning to believe that Kimble was guilty, after all—and yet, something stubborn in him kept reading, kept looking for that unidentifiable bit of information that his intuition insisted was there—insisted that he and everyone else had missed the first time they had gone over it.

Gerard had read through the forty-page transcript once, at a swift and desperate pace; he was now on his second go-round, reading more carefully this time, on page twenty-three.

Kelly: Let's take it from the top again, Dr. Kimble. You got off work, drove to the CRAAF benefit, met your wife there, drove her home . . .

Kimble: Why do we have to keep repeating all this?

Gerard closed his eyes and could hear the precise tone Kimble had used; he already knew beyond any doubt the stricken look Kelly and Rosetti had seen in Kimble's eyes.

Rosetti: Just bear with us, okay?

Kimble: I told you already—I took Helen home, but right as we pulled up, I got a call that Tim Price needed help with a bleeder.

Kelly: You mean another surgeon needed help with a patient in the operating room?

Kimble: (Nods.)

Kelly: About what time was this?

Kimble: God . . . I don't know . . . (inaudible) . . . I can't remember. Maybe . . . ten. Ten-thirty. I don't know . . . It—it must have been after ten, because I didn't get to the benefit until almost eight-thirty, and I know we were there at least an hour and a half, maybe two hours.

God, Helen's family doesn't even know. Can't I . . . can't I call them? Somebody should tell—

Kelly: In a little while, Dr. Kimble. So, you got a call from Tim Price between ten and ten-thirty?

Kimble: Something like that.

Kelly: And you drove to the benefit around eight-thirty?

Kimble: Yeah. Well, no, I didn't drive. I took a cab.

Gerard sat forward at his desk, and read the sentence again.

Kelly: I thought you said you drove Helen home.

Kimble: I did. I loaned a friend of mine—Charlie—Charlie Nichols—I loaned him my car that afternoon so he could run an errand. Just for a few hours.

Kelly: He returned it to you at the benefit?

Kimble: Yeah. He was there. Gave me my keys back—I mean, the valet ticket so I could get them back.

Kelly: Let's go back to when you dropped Helen off at the house . . .

The police radio scanner on the counter behind Gerard emitted a burst of static, causing him to slosh coffee onto the transcript. He swore, found a napkin in the top drawer of his desk, and sopped it up as the message came through, loud enough to be heard down the corridor, loud enough to draw Renfro and Poole out of their nearby offices to listen at his door:

". . . units in the vicinity of Balbo Street Station. Be alert to possible sighting of Richard Kimble . . ."

Gerard rose, heart pounding not in reaction to the caffeine overdose or the information coming over the scanner, but to the words he had just read.

"Balbo Station," Renfro said. "That's—"

Gerard knew precisely where it was, knew precisely why Kimble had gone there, knew precisely why Frederick Sykes had taken pains to give C.P.D. the slip and leave his apartment. He cut Renfro off. "Poole! Get Biggs and Newman."

Accompanied by Renfro and Poole, he ran down

the corridors, down the stairs to the parking garage in the basement.

Renfro drove, with Poole beside him; Biggs and Newman followed in a second sedan. The night was bitterly cold and cloudy, barren of starlight. Gerard sat in the backseat, listening to a mental chorus of voices:

(Not my problem . . .)
(He's innocent, isn't he?
What makes you say that?
You.)
(Do you remember what you said to me?
I remember you were pointing my gun at me . . .)

The first flurries of an encroaching snowstorm began to fall as the report came over the radio:

"All units in vicinity of Balbo El. Officer down. Repeat, officer down. Man leaving scene with two guns matches description of Richard Kimble . . ."

(I didn't kill my wife . . .)

In the front seat, Renfro and Poole listened in electrified silence. *Officer down* meant the entire Chicago police force would be combing the city for Richard Kimble; *officer down* meant they would ask questions later, and shoot first.

Shoot to kill.

"Damn," Gerard whispered, and closed his eyes. If any harm came to Richard Kimble, that blood would stain Gerard's hands for a very long time to come.

13

Kimble fled unnoticed through an underground mall beneath the hotel, slowing only to deposit the guns into a mailbox. He took the escalator up, still moving, taking steps two at a time, and strode into the main lobby of the Chicago Hilton.

A bulletin board on the wall listed hospitality suites and speakers for the Devlin-Macgregor conference. Kimble paused just long enough to read:

"Advances in Nuclear Tissue and
Pathology Research"
Speaker: Dr. Charles Nichols
Grand Ballroom, Rooftop

Kimble caught the elevator and rode up alone.

* * *

By the time Renfro pulled up in front of the Hilton, the police had already cleared the sidewalks. Amazingly, Newman and Biggs were already there and decked out in Kevlar. With Biggs a step behind, Newman hurried over to Gerard and handed him a vest, his expression a mixture of despondence and urgency.

"C.P.D. just reported—"

"I heard," Gerard said shortly. "Was it Kimble?" He did not want to believe Kimble capable of such an act—did not want to think that he was responsible for forcing an innocent man to take a life, but he also knew that Kimble might have been driven to take desperate measures.

Newman looked away and did not answer.

"Conflicting reports," Biggs said, stepping up beside him. "But the cops are considering him a shooter."

Gerard stared as two more police cruisers appeared out of the swirl of snow flurries and pulled up in front of the hotel. Four heavily armed officers crawled out. Gerard headed for the hotel's front entrance and paused just in front of the sliding doors, where Detective Kelly was conferring with a Kevlar-decked C.P.D. captain.

"Witnesses say he entered the hotel from the subway," the captain was saying.

Eyes bright with the excitement of the chase, Kelly gave a short nod. "Okay. I want it locked down. Start on the lower levels."

The captain moved off; Gerard moved in to intercept the detective.

"That's my man in there, Kelly."

Kelly half turned and gazed at the inspector with open contempt, which was secretly returned tenfold. "Not since he took down one of ours, Gerard. This is a police matter now. Stay the hell out of it."

He wheeled and moved off before Gerard could say another word. Gerard watched Kelly's back recede as the police officer headed into the hotel lobby, then gazed up at the hotel roof.

Newman approached, and handed Gerard his belt and backup piece.

"C'mon," Gerard told him. "I know where he's going."

Newman blinked. "How?"

"Call it a hunch," Gerard said, holding the younger man's gaze. "They're never wrong, you know."

Newman tilted his head like a puzzled terrier; by that time, Gerard had already headed into the lobby, and Newman had to run to catch up to him.

Kimble exited the elevator at the rooftop level and followed the signs to the ballroom, moving with ruthless determination. At the closed double doors, a man wearing a jacket with the hotel insignia stepped into his path.

The man glanced at Kimble's chest, seeking a plastic name tag, then smiled politely and said, in a low voice as if confiding a secret, "Sorry, sir. This function is for registered convention guests only—"

Kimble lifted the man under the elbows, set him aside, and flung open the doors.

Inside, Dr. Charles Nichols stood atop a red-draped platform, lecturing to a packed house:

"And I especially would like to thank my researchers who helped me—"

At the sight of Kimble, Nichols broke off and grasped the lectern with both hands, as if to steady himself. Those sitting in the rear of the ballroom turned, frowning at the interruption.

"Richard . . ." Nichols whispered.

Kimble strode down the red-carpeted center aisle toward the dais and, for the first time in a year, raised his voice in a crowd, no longer afraid to be seen. "What's wrong, Charlie? Surprised?"

Nichols stared at him, stricken, unable to reply.

"Sykes couldn't take me down a year ago; what made you think he could take me now?"

The crowd hushed; and then a whisper traveled through the room, from back to front, as Kimble passed familiar faces in the crowd—Jake Roberts, Tim Price, Moh Falawi.

It's him . . . It's Richard Kimble . . .

Kimble looked at them and saw none of them; he saw only Nichols, spoke only to Nichols, as though only they two existed.

"After Lentz died," Kimble said, his voice strong, clear, cutting through the background hum of the crowd, "you were the only one that had access to the pathology reports."

Nichols collected himself, held on to the lectern as

Kimble neared the dais. "Reports?" His expression
was veiled, unreadable. "What're you—"

"You switched the samples and falsified the reports so RDU90 could get approval."

Another ripple passed through the crowd.

Nichols gave a small laugh of disbelief, but his
eyes did not smile. "Richard . . ." He shook his
head, half grinning. "I don't know what you're talking about . . ."

Kimble came to a stop in the aisle in front of the
lectern and stared up at Nichols with white, cold
fury. "I have a set of the original samples."

He was close enough now to read Nichols's eyes,
close enough to see them narrow, to detect the flicker
of concern. "You almost pulled it off, Charlie. But I
know all about it now, and I can prove it."

The two men held a look; and then Nichols turned
to the audience, hand out in an appeal for under-
standing. "Ladies and gentlemen . . . My . . . friend,
as you can see, is obviously not well." He stepped
back from the microphone and said, in the same pa-
tronizing tone that Walter Gutherie had used, "Richard, if you want to talk—"

"I didn't come here to talk."

Nichols drew back slightly at the hatred coiled in
the other man's voice and posture, then began to
move across the dais toward the side exit. Kimble
paralleled him, passing tables, groups of shocked, silent spectators, and followed Nichols out the door.

Outside in the corridor, Nichols broke into a run
and headed into a hospitality suite. Kimble entered it
three steps behind—and staggered back, then

dropped, felled by the pain and impact of a hurled chair.

He got to his hands and knees just as Nichols circled behind him and locked the door.

And then Nichols was on him again, pulling him by the front of his jacket to his feet before he could get his balance. For an instant, he met Charlie's eyes, and was stunned by the depth of the coldness there, by the sudden hideousness that contorted Charlie's handsome face.

I don't know you, Kimble thought. *I never did know you . . .*

Nichols thrust his face into Kimble's. "Your best quality, Richard, is that you don't give up, even when it's in your best interest to . . ."

He slammed Kimble backwards again, driving him past the outer suite into a conference library. Kimble reeled, fought to regain his bearings, but Charlie was on him again, driving a fist into his stomach, hurling him against a fire exit.

"I always knew I'd have to kill you," Nichols hissed. "Now, I must thank you for giving me two hundred witnesses tonight who will support me when I tell them it was self-defense . . ."

They grappled. The fire doors opened behind Kimble, and he stumbled backwards onto a fire escape, feet giving way under him. At the last minute, he clutched the railing and looked behind him, to see that he was dangling on the edge of the escape some twenty floors above the street.

A blur in the periphery of his vision; he glanced up to see Nichols diving for him. At the last minute, he rolled, and knocked Charlie back against the opposite railing. The rooftop lights illumined the darkness behind Nichols, revealing a slow, steady rain of snow.

"You missed your chance, Charlie," Kimble gasped.

Nichols charged. Kimble lashed out, connected with two blows that sent Nichols hurtling down a half flight of stairs. He dashed down after him.

Nichols rose unsteadily, took a dizzy swing. Kimble landed another blow, and cried, "You took everything away from me . . . for money . . . !"

Nichols landed on all fours on the rooftop. Kimble scrambled after, pulled the other man to his feet, spoke softly into Nichols's ear.

"I want to know, Charlie . . . was it worth it?"

Silhouetted by the glittering city skyline, Nichols's head wobbled; blood and saliva trickled from his split lip, but his expression was unyielding, coldly determined. "This thing is bigger than even you think, Richard. You can't stop it."

Kimble made a noise of pure rage and struck out with stunning force. Nichols was hurled against one of the parapets that lined the rooftop's edge, and turned his face to stare down, terrified, at the miniature police cars lining the snow-dusted street below.

Kimble moved to him, grasped his lapels with a sense of unhappy triumph. It would be easy, so easy, to strike another blow that sent Nichols over the edge, to listen with pleasure to his scream as he fell . . .

Rhythmic thunder pounded in his ears. He looked

up, blinded, into dazzling white light and heard rather than saw the chopper. A voice boomed overhead:

"Chicago police. Freeze . . ."

Kimble froze. In that instant of uncertainty, Nichols saw his chance, kneed his opponent in the chest, and fled.

Minutes earlier, Gerard, Newman, and Poole moved through the hotel lobby toward the main bank of elevators; Biggs hurried to join them. "C.P.D. has the perimeter," he said, adjusting his Kevlar vest. "Hotel security has the parking structure."

"Let them keep busy down below," Gerard said. He paused at the directory, saw the location of the speech given by Charles Nichols, and turned to Newman. "Newman, get with security. See if you can locate Kimble from the monitors. Keep in radio contact."

Newman nodded and hurried off swiftly, his movements once again eager, hopeful.

Gerard and the others headed over to the light-trimmed glass elevators. They trooped onto the first available one, and when Gerard pressed the button for the rooftop, Poole and Biggs, who were studying a schematic of the hotel, frowned quizzically at him.

Around the fourteenth floor, as Gerard stared down at moving figures—now the size of currants—on the lobby level, his radio squawked.

"Gerard."

"It's Newman. I've got Kimble on the roof with Nichols. Southeast exit."

"Keep an eye on him," Gerard ordered.

Behind him, Poole demanded, "How'd you do that?"

Gerard permitted himself a small, tight smile.

"There are four exits to the roof," Biggs said, looking up from the schematic.

"I want them covered."

Biggs nodded, and picked up his radio.

When they reached the rooftop level, the elevator opened to a crowd of panicked conventiongoers seeking escape. Gerard drew a breath and waded into the confusion. He found two security guards who knew the way to the rooftop exit; they led him down the corridors to a hospitality suite, where two concerned conventioneers were trying to force open the locked door.

One of them glanced up at Gerard and the uniformed guards. "We think Kimble followed Charles Nichols in here."

"Get that door open," Gerard ordered, and waited, impatient, while one of the security men fished out a key and unlocked the door.

Inside the suite lay signs of a struggle: two overturned chairs, and an open door leading out to the roof. Gerard ran to the doorway, then paused and turned toward the guards. Kimble had enough on his hands without having to deal with would-be heroes. "Stay at this door."

The vehemence in his tone convinced the two

guards; they nodded, and watched as Gerard made his way out onto the rooftop alone.

The exit opened onto three flights of metal fire stairs, which in turn led down to the flat rooftop. Gerard narrowed his eyes against the sting of windborne snow and the million-candlepower glare of helicopter lights. He hurried down the steps, careful not to slip on the white powder accumulating there, unable to hear anything other than the howl of winter wind and the roar of the police chopper.

Gerard knew what was happening inside the chopper; a sharpshooter was working to get Kimble in his sights. He squinted into the beam and saw Nichols, running, and Kimble going after him.

An easy target.

Gerard pulled out his radio. Before he could raise it, bullets sprayed the rooftop, bounced singing off concrete, tore through the air-conditioning ducts where Kimble had stood not one second before.

Gerard dove to the bottom of the fire escape and stayed until he was sure the barrage had ceased.

"Kimble!"

He wanted to tell Kimble to stay on Nichols, for protection, but the wind threw his voice back at him, and the deafening thrum of the chopper drowned out his words. He lifted the radio to his lips and screamed into it as he pushed himself to his feet.

"This is a United States marshal! Get that helicopter out of here!"

But Kimble's moving silhouette remained encircled by the dazzling beam, awhirl with glittering white snow. Gerard followed as Kimble darted around blowing heat vents and duct work, relentlessly gaining ground on Nichols's crouched, fleeing form. Renfro's voice filtered through the radio in his jacket:

"There's a U.S. marshal out there! Hold your fire!"

The beam's circumference shrank as the chopper retreated, pulling up. Nichols headed toward the shadows near the roof's edge; Kimble surged forward and tackled him, causing them both to lose their footing and fall against the sloped glass roof of an elevator housing.

The lights trimming the elevators illuminated the shaft; in their faint glow, Gerard watched the two dark figures wrestle on the glass as he approached. Above, the helicopter circled, searching, then cast its spotlight on the two struggling men, and Gerard approaching.

Empowered by rage, Kimble slammed Nichols down against the housing. The glass buckled beneath the man's weight. Kimble reached down, pulled Nichols up, slammed him down again.

Again.

Again.

Gerard propelled himself to the edge of the elevator housing, gun drawn, and shouted with all his strength, forcing every last molecule of air from his lungs. "Kimble . . . !"

Again.

The glass gave in a sparkling cascade as brilliant, as glitteringly beautiful as the snow. Kimble and Nichols fell away.

Aghast, Gerard peered over the edge of the shattered housing and down. He caught only the briefest glimpse of Kimble, clinging to the broken roof of a glass elevator, before the car descended into darkness.

Gerard holstered his weapon and tore across the rooftop, half slipping over the snow as he ran. At the fire exit, Renfro joined him, and the two dashed down the back stairwell as Gerard barked into his radio. "Where did the elevator stop?"

The half second's pause seemed too long; Gerard opened his mouth to yell again into the speaker grid when Newman answered, his voice high-pitched with excitement:

"Level five. Laundry and maintenance, no guest rooms."

It was a long way down. Gerard's chest was heaving by the time he and Renfro made it to the fifth floor. On the stairwell, both drew their weapons—Gerard his Glock, Renfro his .38—then paused in front of the fire door. Gerard spoke into his radio.

"We're going in. Give me five minutes. Tell Biggs to keep C.P.D. out."

He nodded at Renfro, and the two of them slammed against the door.

The door opened. Gerard peered into the dimly lit, steamy mists of a cavernous industrial laundry room. Swinging quarter-ton canvas bags screeched along ceiling tracks, groaning metallically as they dumped piles of dirty laundry onto conveyor belts, which in turn led to two thunderous thirty-foot-long washers.

At the entrance, two women stood sorting laundry

onto a small conveyor; they glanced up, startled, as Gerard and Renfro entered with guns drawn.

"Get out of here," Gerard told them, and the women wasted no time complying. He and Renfro cautiously rounded a corner and found another laundry worker, a man, hooking one of the huge canvas bags onto the overhead rail via a hydraulic lift, which raised the bag on a yellow steel I-beam.

The man took one look at the guns and disappeared before anyone could say a word.

Gerard headed into the main laundry area and motioned for Renfro to take the far side, while Gerard moved up the room's center.

Gerard raised his voice, loud enough to cut through the sounds of squealing metal, thrashing water. "Kimble! There's no way out of here! The building is locked down."

He kept advancing, moving carefully through an obstacle course of hanging canvas bags, metal tracks, conveyor belts, equipment. He could sense Kimble's presence, knew that the man was listening; with a deeply felt sincerity that he prayed would convey itself in his tone, he shouted, "Kimble! I know about Nichols. I know about Sykes . . ."

In the dim, steamy silence, broken only by the whir of machinery, he imagined he could hear Kimble hesitating, thinking.

Not my problem . . .

I'm just the poor working man who's paid to hunt you down.

And knew that what he had just said would not be enough.

A bag slid suddenly, swiftly, down the track toward him. Gerard spun to one side, dodging it nimbly, then called out again. "Nichols borrowed your car the night of the murder. We know he called Sykes from your car . . ."

Kimble might believe him now; but so would any others who might be listening. As he moved into the open area between the conveyor belts, Gerard maintained vigilance, ready to pivot and shoot at a second's notice—and realizing that any threat to his life now came not from Richard Kimble, but from the all-too-perfect Dr. Charles Nichols.

". . . That's why there was no forced entry at your house," Gerard said. "He had used your keys."

He moved forward slowly between the two gigantic industrial washers, their ten-foot-high sides forming a stainless-steel alleyway, and delivered his final plea.

"Kimble! It's time to quit running . . ."

Kimble moved under cover of the bags and laundry carts near the conveyor belts, only a short distance from Gerard, and listened.

When he had first realized Nichols was the killer, madness had seized him. He had wanted nothing more than to hurt Nichols; and now that he was coming to himself, he wanted only to capture Nichols, to force him to confess. The forged reports, the falsified slides, all pointed to Nichols. As head of pathology, he alone had the ability to pull the deception off.

Yet every bit of evidence Kimble had was circumstantial; and without Nichols's and Sykes's confessions, he had nothing to concretely tie them to Helen's murder other than his own testimony—the testimony of a convicted killer. Proving that Nichols was involved in a deception to gain approval for a dangerous drug did not prove that he had ordered Sykes to murder Kimble.

Kimble had made a decision: either he would force a confession out of Charlie Nichols, or he would die trying.

Yet on the rooftop, as he had wrestled with Nichols, something puzzling had happened. He had thought himself dead when bullets had started raining down from the helicopter—but the bullets had ceased.

Then Gerard had appeared, with his weapon drawn, and Kimble had known once again that he was about to die; the marshal had had several chances to aim and shoot Kimble before he caught up to the fleeing Nichols.

Amazingly, Gerard had not fired. Instead, he had called out to him—and now Kimble crouched behind glistening steel machinery and listened as Gerard called out to him again.

I know about Nichols. I know about Sykes . . .

Easy enough for Gerard to say. Kimble had made it clear enough that he was trying to implicate Sykes and Nichols; he decided Gerard was merely trying to placate him.

And yet—a small seed of doubt began to germinate. Gerard had not fired when he had the chance.

Even so, Kimble had kept moving then, looking

for Nichols. There was probably no way out of the surrounded building—from the rooftop, he had seen the police cruisers lining the streets below. But he intended to find Nichols, use him as a shield, use Charlie's fear of death to force a public confession from him. If he could get to Charlie, there was a small chance he could make it out alive.

If not, he would still keep running. Death from a hail of bullets was likely to be swift, if not clean.

And then Gerard had said: *Nichols borrowed your car the night of the murder. We know he called Sykes from your car.*

Kimble slowed, hesitated. Wanted to believe.

Gerard could have been lying about the call to Sykes; but he was not lying about Nichols's borrowing the car, and to know that, Gerard would have had to go through the arrest report.

Gerard had checked.

Not my problem—

Kimble took a faltering step, still wary, still keeping an eye out for Nichols, but the realization that Gerard had considered—had *checked*—struck home.

And then Gerard called out a third time.

That's why there was no forced entry at your house. He'd used your keys . . .

Kimble took a step backward and sagged against a steam-dampened wall as he released a silent sob. For the past year, he had never understood how Sykes had managed to slip into his house without a trace, with the doors still locked when Helen, then Kimble arrived home . . . In the heat of his fury at Charlie, the simple explanation had never occurred to him.

Nor would it have occurred to Gerard, unless he believed in Nichols's guilt.

Kimble! It's time to quit running . . .

He rose and began to move toward the sound of Gerard's voice.

In the meantime, on the other side of the room, Renfro cautiously worked his way through the maze of machinery. He was not terrified for his life—he had been through too many situations like this one with Gerard, and many worse—but he was distinctly nervous. True, Kimble was not armed at the moment, but he had seen and heard of deputies killed because they blithely assumed they would maintain the advantage. With someone as desperate as Kimble, anything could happen.

Renfro wheeled at a *swoosh*ing noise; behind him, one of the quarter-ton bags came sailing down the ceiling track, with enough speed and momentum to snap a man's neck. With a dancer's grace, Renfro quickly angled his upper torso to one side, avoiding collision at the last instant.

When Gerard began to call out to Kimble, Renfro listened carefully—not just to his boss's words, but for sounds of Kimble's movement nearby.

Kimble . . . I know about Nichols. I know about Sykes . . .

Renfro thought nothing of the statement. As Gerard so often advised, he did not concern himself with his prey's guilt or innocence; he was only concerned with bringing Kimble in, and he assumed that

Gerard's words were nothing more than a clever appeal designed to trick Kimble into surrendering himself.

Yet when Gerard said, *Nichols borrowed your car the night of the murder. We know he called Sykes from your car,* Renfro listened, puzzled.

He had not understood why Gerard had risked going out on the roof, had not just allowed the sharpshooters in the chopper to bring Kimble down. He had believed, along with Poole, that Kimble's attempts to implicate Sykes were (a) nothing more than an effort to distract the marshals from the real target of their search or (b) an effort to get even with the hit man who got off scot-free.

The business with Nichols he did not understand at all; and though he kept moving, kept scanning for Kimble, Renfro paused mentally to consider whether Gerard might actually have meant what he said. He had, after all, been reading Kimble's arrest transcript when the word had come from C.P.D., and he had been strangely preoccupied on the drive to the Hilton—

That's why there was no forced entry at your house. He'd used your keys . . .

And that statement brought Renfro up short, because it was the first time he had ever heard an explanation for the lack of forced entry other than Kimble's guilt.

It caused no more than a split-second gap in Renfro's attention, and in that gap, another canvas bag came whizzing at him. Renfro ducked; the bag grazed the top of his head, tousling his hair, but he straightened, unscathed, and released a sigh.

And spun around at the *whirr* behind him.

He turned too late, but in the split second before he lost consciousness, he caught in his peripheral vision a flash of the yellow steel I-beam hurtling toward impact with his skull, and behind it the advancing form of Charles Nichols.

14

Kimble! It's time to quit running . . .

Kimble moved around the carts toward the huge steel washing machines and the sound of Gerard's voice—and stopped at the sight of an unconscious man sprawled across the floor where the canvas bags tracked.

He dropped to his knees and crawled over to him, ducking as another giant canvas laundry bag swung through the air at them. When the bag passed, Kimble dragged the man—according to the I.D. on his jacket, a U.S. marshal—away from the tracks and knelt beside him to quickly examine him.

No injuries other than the obvious one, a bleeding gash on the side of his head. Kimble probed it swiftly, gently, and found no depressed bone fragments.

(Don't think of Helen. Not now . . . there isn't time . . .)

Pulse was strong and steady; breathing was good. Kimble gently lifted the man's eyelids with the tip of his thumb, and bent forward, squinting in the dim light.

Pupils both the same size, contracting slightly. Probably just a concussion, and he would come to soon. In the E.R., they would have kept him a few hours after he woke for observation, just to be sure.

But the most ominous sight was the man's empty shoulder holster. Kimble looked up, realizing that Nichols had to be close by, had to have the gun.

Gerard called out again, nearer this time.

"Kimble! If you don't come out . . . you know I'll stop you . . ."

Kimble crouched low and moved stealthily toward the sound of his pursuer's voice, making his way alongside one of the endless stainless-steel washers, past abandoned carts, past long metal poles used to push wet laundry from the washers onto the conveyors.

He came to the edge of one of the washers and stopped, still in shadow, still hidden from view. A few feet away to his left, Gerard moved slowly in the corridor formed by the two long washers, gun held at the ready. The marshal paused, glanced over his shoulder, then turned his back to the rear wall, unaware of Kimble beside him.

As he did, Charlie Nichols glided silently out behind him and took aim with the stolen weapon.

Kimble grabbed one of the twenty-foot poles and

shouted, instinctively using the nickname he had given Nichols long ago, when they were both interns. "Hey, Chuckles!"

Nichols whirled, ready to kill.

Kimble swung with all his strength, all his anger, all his grief. The pole caught Nichols alongside the neck, throwing him off balance, dashing his forehead against the steel edge of the washer with a solid *thunk*. He crumpled and slid into an unconscious heap; the gun dropped from his hand and skittered across the floor.

At the instant Nichols fell, Gerard spun around, gun raised. Kimble stepped forward—into the light, into the line of fire—and leaned wearily against the pole in his hands.

For an icy millisecond Kimble watched as Gerard teetered on the brink of instinct, on the verge of shooting at what seemed to be the nearest available threat—Kimble; and in that millisecond, the marshal's eyes were breathtakingly cold, free of the regret they had held when he had fired upon Kimble at the federal lockup.

Kimble considered that perhaps everything Gerard had said about Charlie and the car keys had been a lie, designed to entrap. Or perhaps Gerard knew the truth, but simply did not care.

Not my problem . . .

Charlie had been a liar and a killer, and Kimble had been foolish enough to trust him. Perhaps Kimble was foolish to trust Gerard now—and now Gerard would kill him.

He did not care. He sagged, spent, against the laundry pole.

All of this passed in less than a second, and then Gerard stopped himself and caught sight of Nichols's still form. The coldness in his eyes faded, replaced by a deep relief that Kimble did not understand. Gerard began to lower the gun, but hesitated, uncertain.

Kimble did not move.

Slowly, Gerard holstered his weapon, reached for his radio, spoke into the grid.

"Open it up. It's over."

Within seconds, the room swarmed with marshals and Chicago police and hotel security, all of them armed, most of them wearing bulletproof vests.

Kimble kept looking for Gerard's eyes, but the inspector disappeared into a sudden surge of Chicago police. Kimble understood; they believed he had killed the cop on the el. They had a score to settle. Perhaps Gerard believed it too.

They aimed their weapons at Kimble and made him drop the pole and raise his arms; they ignored him when he told them the injured marshal had a concussion. They simply told him to hold out his hands, then cuffed him. Prodded him, ordered him, made him move, escorted by men and women with guns and hardened expressions, onto the elevator, down through the lobby, where through the glass doors he watched as Charlie Nichols, strapped to a gurney, was loaded into the back of an ambulance.

The doors opened to bitter cold. Surrounded by a

sea of uniformed bodies, Kimble stepped out onto the snow-laden sidewalk where wind swirled the last lingering flurries of the storm. There were reporters, newsvans, camera flashes, and TV lights that blinded him, reflected dazzlingly off the white sidewalks.

Kimble kept his head down, kept his gaze fastened on the snow. Kept moving as he passed people standing in the glare of television lights, and heard snatches of reports:

—saga of once-prominent Chicago surgeon, Doctor Richard Kimble, who escaped from an Illinois Corrections bus, took a strange twist this evening—

—unconfirmed reports from police of new evidence which may exonerate Kimble while implicating some of the biggest names in medicine—

—didn't know what he was going to do. My wife was very frightened. The next thing I knew, cops—

A woman clutching a microphone broke through the barrier created by Kimble's grim-faced entourage and shouted, "Doctor Kimble, is it true you can prove your innocence?"

"Get them back," a familiar voice snapped, and Kimble glanced up to see that Gerard now flanked him. The tide of uniformed bodies surged forward past them, and cleared a path toward a waiting sedan. A tall, broad-shouldered marshal opened the back door and gestured for Kimble to get in.

"Watch your head, Doctor Kimble," he said softly, and Kimble stared at him, startled by the gratuitous courtesy, by the respect he saw in the man's gaze. As Kimble climbed into the backseat, his balance uncertain because of his cuffed hands, the man caught his elbow to steady him, then closed the door.

An eager-faced young man sat behind the steering wheel, and, as Gerard slipped into the front seat beside him, shared a complicitous look with the inspector that Kimble could not fathom. He was no longer sure what to expect; he could not tell from the marshals' stone-faced, impassive gaze whether Gerard thought him guilty of the transit cop's murder or not, but he felt relieved to be far away from the noise and the lights. He leaned exhausted against the seat.

Gerard rolled down the front window and motioned to someone in the crowd. "Poole! You got that thing?"

A black woman moved up to the window, handed Gerard something square, blue. Gerard took it, rolled up the window, turned toward Kimble.

"Give me your hands."

Kimble hesitated, then held up his cuffed wrists. Gerard unlocked the cuffs, set them on the front seat, then placed the square blue object on the doctor's bruised hands. Kimble winced at the sensation of burning cold and realized it was an ice pack.

A curious lightness crept into the inspector's voice and expression. "Take care of those hands, Doc. You're going to need them again soon."

Kimble stared at him, overwhelmed by the realization that Gerard believed him—that what he had said about Nichols had all been true. And if Gerard believed him, he would not rest until he saw Nichols convicted, and Kimble freed.

He looked down at the ice pack on his battered

hands, then back up at Gerard and said dully, "I thought you told me you didn't care."

In the rearview's reflection, the young driver beamed at both of them.

Gerard sensed it and went wooden again, breaking off eye contact. "Yeah, well . . ." There was a faint awkwardness in his tone that brought Kimble to the edge of a smile. "Don't spread it around."

He met Kimble's gaze again. Kimble hesitated as he studied the marshal's face, wanting to express his gratitude, his relief, wanting to say something—and found himself unable to speak.

Gerard seemed to understand; the corner of his mouth quirked, and then he turned and settled back in his seat.

Unseen, Kimble smiled and leaned wearily back to gaze out the window at the street lamps moving past. It was then he realized for the first time that the wind and snow had ceased. The clouds had cleared, leaving a skyful of stars, and the night was perfectly still.